WORLDS APART

Jill Murphy produced her first book at the tender age of six and completed her bestseller, *The Worst Witch*, while still only eighteen. It wasn't until six years later, though, that the book was finally accepted and published. During this time, she worked in a children's home and as a nanny – "I enjoyed it so much," she says, "I very nearly became a social worker."

She wrote and  Witch stories, *T* and *A Bad Spell* three titles have *Worlds Apart*, th central characters are based on a mother and daughter whom the author knows, and much of the setting is on and around London's Hampstead Heath, near where Jill once lived. "The stories I like, are stories that sound as though they really happened," she says.

Jill Murphy's most recent fiction title is *Geoffrey Strangeways* (Walker Books, 1990) and she has also written and illustrated several picture books, including *Five Minutes' Peace* (1987 Best Book for Babies), *All in One Piece* (commended for the 1987 Kate Greenaway Medal), *A Piece of Cake* – all published by W

Books by the same author

The Worst Witch
The Worst Witch Strikes Again
A Bad Spell for the Worst Witch

Picture books:
Peace at Last
On the Way Home
Whatever Next!
Five Minutes' Peace
All in One Piece

WORLDS APART

JILL MURPHY

WALKER BOOKS
LONDON

First published 1988 by Walker Books Ltd
87 Vauxhall Walk, London SE11 5HJ

This edition published 1990

Printed in Great Britain by Cox and Wyman Ltd, Reading
Typeset in Hong Kong by Graphicraft Typesetters Ltd

British Library Cataloguing in Publication Data
Murphy, Jill
Worlds apart.
I. Title
823'.914 [J]   PZ7
ISBN 0-7445-1475-4

For Naomi Russell
with tons of love

CHAPTER ONE

First of all before I begin, just let me tell you a few things about myself. I mean, it could be anyone writing this couldn't it? As far as *you* know, I could be a man or a woman, a doctor, a train driver, a ballet dancer, a lion tamer – oh, anything at all – and I could be very old or very young.

Well, after all those exciting possibilities, the truth is that I'm just a schoolgirl and I'm nearly twelve. I'm good at reading and writing and hopeless at everything else and that's just about it really. A bit of a let down, isn't it?

And to crown this thrilling description, I have to add that I'm not in the least bit pretty. I do so wish I was, but there doesn't seem to be much hope in that direction, though friends try to be kind about it.

Now I don't want to give you the impression that I never think about anything else but me, but I'll just give you a detailed description of what I look like and then I can get on with the story.

Hair first: straightish with a kink at the end. It's mousy-coloured and sometimes it has a distinctly olive-green tint – honestly, I'm not exaggerating. I grew it so that I could have plaits, but it was only long enough this year and now I'm too old for plaits, so I wear it loose or in a pony-tail.

Eyebrows: two fat, furry caterpillars marching in a straight line across my forehead.

Nose: indescribable.

Mouth: cavernous. When I smile, it practically goes round the back of my head.

Eyes: not bad at all considering everything else. They're greyish-green (like the hair!).

7

It looks as if I'm going to be at least seven feet tall by the time I've finished growing, though by some miracle I have very small hands and feet. Still, there's plenty of time for them to sprout to size eighty-nine shoes and great mangling hands.

Oh, by the way, I bite my fingernails, so the tiny hands don't look very appealing at the moment. I really am making a determined effort to stop though. I bought some revolting stuff from the chemist which I paint on my nails every morning. It tastes absolutely foul and it's supposed to be guaranteed to put you off biting them, but it doesn't seem to work with me. When you're addicted you just grit your teeth and chew away, whatever it tastes like.

By the way, I forgot to mention that I have reasonably nice white teeth and I've got freckles. To say that I'm afflicted with freckles would be a better way of putting it. They go right into my hairline, and the whole impression is that some lunatic has sprayed my face with brown paint.

Mother has thick, black, curly hair, the same eyes as me only greyer and she is tiny and slim and pretty. I thought I'd sneak that description of Mother in, and that is positively the last description before I begin the actual story.

Sorry about this, just three more things. I sing very well, I'm good at drawing and I'm batty about animals. I have a goldfish and, at the moment, a jar full of snails, which I'm setting free tomorrow because it's cruel to keep them too long, and one of my ambitions is to have a dog, a huge, furry, sloppy dog who loves me, but they aren't allowed at the flat where we live.

That's *it*. The story begins in the next chapter, I promise.

CHAPTER TWO

I wonder if you've noticed that I haven't mentioned my father yet? It must seem odd that I haven't given you a description of him, particularly as I've been raving on for hours about what I look like.

The reason I haven't mentioned him is that up until a few weeks ago I had no idea who he was. Mother never spoke about him at all – he was a subject not to be mentioned.

When I was about two or three years old, I remember asking her why I didn't have a daddy like the other children at playschool. She replied that I was different from the other children and I didn't need a daddy because I had a nice, devoted mummy and she didn't want to hear another word about it. So she didn't hear another word about it, but of course I still thought about it. It seemed a bit like the situation in the Garden of Eden. You know, when Adam and Eve were having a wonderful time, and everything was happy and just right, but there was that one tree that they weren't allowed to go near, so they started thinking about it all the time. Well, Mother and I had a marvellous time together, except when I was naughty of course – like all little kids are – but I couldn't help wondering about that one person who she just wouldn't talk about.

Now I shall have to give you a little information about the early days of my life, or none of the rest of this story will make sense.

I'll start from when I was about three, because I can't really remember very well before then. Mother was an actress in those days. She went on being an actress until I was about eight, oh and I did love it all. She used to take me to rehearsals, and all the other actors and stagehands used to spoil me to death. I was always curled up on some nice person's lap, or riding on someone's shoulders, or being stuffed with crisps and biscuits.

As a special treat they used to let me dress up in the costumes, or paint my face with grease-paint. I remember once getting very attached (literally!) to a purple feather boa which I insisted on wearing all the time. I even wore it home on the bus, much to the delight of the other passengers. Mother's got a photo of me wearing it in our album.

Mother wasn't in any of the big shows in London, and she never got a good part on the television, though she was in a soap advert once when I was a tiny baby. She always seemed to be in shows that went touring all over the country and she was always worrying about whether to take me with her or leave me with friends; anyway, to cut a long story short, she suddenly decided that she didn't want to be an actress any more and got a job working in a little dress shop at the end of the road.

I tried my best to make her stay in the theatre, but she wouldn't hear of it. Once Mother's mind is made up that's *it*. It's like talking to a brick wall, and if you "keep on" about whatever it is she just gets irritable. She can't stand people "keeping on".

I think she decided to give it up because she was worried about me being dragged round to all the theatres in my school holidays and sitting through the endless rehearsals. I *told* her that I enjoyed it all, but she insisted that it was about time I had a proper childhood, with nice clothes and ordinary friends instead of grown-ups all the time. She told me that the long spells out of work meant that we could never save any money, and anyway she'd made up her mind, so would I kindly stop asking her about it?

It's sad really, because another reason why she gave it up was so that she could save enough to rent us a nicer flat than the one we were in, but we're still here three years later. *I* don't mind, although it is a bit gloomy and it *would* be nice to have a garden, but I know that Mother would give anything to have a house with an upstairs and downstairs and a garden to grow vegetables in.

Also, she was much happier before she went to work in the shop. She had a sort of brightness in the old days which just isn't there any more.

She's a manageress at the shop now, so she gets a reasonable amount of money, and the couple who run the shop, Ruth and Martin, are very nice.

It's a nice little shop, very dimly lit, with the clothes hanging on hat stands, and a big, squashy sofa for tired husbands to sit on while their wives try things on. Mother and Ruth have become very good friends which makes it nice for Mother, otherwise it could be rather awful being stuck in the shop all week.

I've just realized that after all you know about my appearance, I forgot to tell you my name. It's Susan. Boring, isn't it? That's because Mother's name is Petunia (Pet for short) and she hates it and didn't want me to be lumbered with a fancy name. I suppose if *her* name had been Susan, she would have wanted *me* to have an interesting name instead of a boring one! I'd rather be Petunia than Susan any day. Well, perhaps not Petunia, but at least Miranda or Victoria or something.

CHAPTER THREE

On Saturdays, Mother's at the shop until one in the afternoon. It doesn't close till six, but Ruth lets her go early because of me. Now that I'm older, I've told her that I don't mind if she stays for the whole day, but I know that she likes to be with me as much as she can. If she worked all day on Saturday, we'd only really see each other on Sunday. I usually meet her at the shop and we go and have lunch together.

One Saturday, I spent the morning with my best friend Zöe. Now there's a lovely name, and those dots over the o are so nice. Actually she's not just my best friend, she's my only friend as well. We go around so much together that I've never got to know anyone else.

Now, this is where it gets extremely difficult to keep to the point, because I shall have to tell you a bit about the Heath, oh, and I've just remembered something else, I haven't even told you which city I live in. Well it's London, and the part where I live is about twenty minutes fast walking from Hampstead Heath.

Hampstead Heath is like a great chunk of rough countryside stuck in the middle of London, and that's about all you need to know really.

So there we were, Zöe and I, out on the Heath on a Saturday morning with our imaginary dogs. I *know* we're a bit old for things like that, and Zöe's already twelve and a month, but we're very young for our age (and proud of it!) and this is our last fling before we start all the business of boys (euk!) and make-up and all that sort of thing.

Zöe has long, frizzy, bright orange hair and a very

white skin and pale eyelashes, and looks even worse than I do. We are, as everyone is always pointing out, a right pair!

My dog is called Loki (that's the god of mischief from *The Heroes of Asgaard*) and Zöe's is named Caliban (after the creature in *The Tempest* by William Shakespeare). Mine is an Irish wolfhound and Zöe's is a husky. They are both beautifully trained and walk to heel, unless we allow them to run ahead and clear the path of wolves and other dangerous creatures.

It was a chilly day, though the month was June which is supposed to be flaming, and we both had our anoraks on. We took the dogs to one of the ponds and threw sticks for them.

"I wish they were real," said Zöe sadly, breaking the spell. "If only we could see them, I mean, really."

"*I* can," I said, feeling a bit cross with her. "Look! Cal got that one and Loki's after that duck on the bank, the one asleep with its leg tucked up under it. It must be deaf if it can't hear Loki sloshing about like a herd of elephants!"

"It can't hear because there aren't any dogs *there*," said Zöe.

She turned and began to walk off down the path. I trotted after her, feeling a bit crushed.

"What's the matter, Zöe?" I asked.

"Oh *I* don't know," she replied. "I'm just not in the mood for them today, that's all."

I looked at my watch (it's a Mickey Mouse one that I've had since I was six but it still works perfectly) and saw that it was time to meet Mother for lunch.

Zöe's mother is a school dinner lady, and her father is an underground train driver. They seem a lot older than my mother and, although they sometimes invite each other round for coffee, they always call each other Mrs Hunter (that's my mother) and Mrs Rawlings (that's Zöe's mum). Zöe also has three brothers, all younger than herself and she doesn't like any of them.

"Can you come out tomorrow?" I asked. "I'll have to be off now so I can meet Mum."

"Can't," replied Zöe. "It's Father's Day tomorrow and we've all got to *do* things for Dad. I'm not quite sure what, but Mum wants us all to be at home. Lucky you, I suppose you'll be allowed out all day."

I smiled and said goodbye, and snapped my fingers for Loki to come with me.

It was very strange, but for the first time ever, I felt upset that I didn't have a father to do things for on Father's Day. I didn't feel lucky at all.

Over the years, many remarks had been made about my lack of father, mainly out of simple curiosity, and I had never minded before. But for some reason on that particular day, I had a very strong feeling of being different from everyone else in a lonely, left out sort of way.

I left Loki at the edge of the Heath. He lives there wild, like a fox or a badger, hidden from the ordinary people. I am the only person who can see him.

Mother was serving a customer in the gloomy little shop. The customer was a tall, thin lady with long, straight blonde hair. She was trying on a beautiful silver dress, cut like a medieval damsel's gown, with flowing, pointed sleeves.

"Do you think it's a bit too extreme for an office party?" the lady was asking my mother.

"*I* think you look lovely in it," I butted in before I'd thought about it, then went very red in the face.

The lady was pleased. "Why, thank you," she said,

smiling at me.

Mother took my arm and drew me towards her. "Hello, darling," she said. "I didn't notice you come in."

The lady had disappeared back into the changing room.

"Where shall we go for lunch today?" asked Mother. It was a joke question as we always go to the same place.

"How about – um, er, perhaps The Harlequin?" I replied. "I've heard they do a very nice sausage and chips there.'

We both laughed.

Mother was wearing a blue T-shirt with WONDER WOMAN emblazoned across the front and a pair of very old, patched jeans. Her hair was tied back in a pony-tail with tendrils of black curls escaping on to her slender neck.

I could see us both reflected in the mirror and, as usual, the difference between us seemed ridiculous. I just don't look anything like her at all.

The lady came out of the changing room and handed Mother the silver dress.

"I'll take it," she said.

Ruth loomed up from a shadowy corner.

"Off you go, you two," she said to us. "I'll wrap this up."

Mother put on her jacket – it's an ancient green one, with red binding round the edges and red buttons, which she's had as long as I can remember – and we set off for The Harlequin.

It touches me, the way she sometimes looks at me as if I'm the most marvellous person in the whole world.

CHAPTER FOUR

It's always seemed very odd to me that Mother never got married again. She's only thirty-three and she's absolutely *barmy* about children, so you'd think she'd have married someone else by now, wouldn't you?

Of course there have been various "uncles" since I was a little girl...well, four to be exact, at least, four *major* uncles if you see what I mean. I won't bother with the minor ones or it'll go on for pages and pages.

Joey was the first one and the longest lasting, from when I was four till I was six. I did like him so much.

He was tall and thin in a shambling, scarecrowy way, and he had those nice, crinkly lines round his eyes that made him look ever so kind. He *was* ever so kind and, most wonderful of all, he had a dog. It was only a tiny Yorkshire terrier but he used to let me hold its lead when we went round the park on Sundays, and sometimes he let me tie a bow on top of its head.

Joey was an actor too. He was in lots of plays with Mother. One of them was a pantomime, and I was often at the theatre during that time, watching the rehearsals or hanging about in the wings while the performance was on. Mother played an old lady and Joey was a chimney sweep. He used to chase me about and try to catch me with his blackened hands and of course I used to giggle my head off. He had very bright blue eyes, and I can still remember them, looking bluer than ever in his sooty face.

He always arrived at our flat on an ancient, rusty bicycle with Tiny (the dog) in a basket on the front. He even fitted a little seat on the back so he could take me for rides too.

Then he didn't come any more. Mother got cross when I asked her about him, so I stopped asking, but I did miss him. I expect Mother thinks I've forgotten him, but I haven't. He was the best yet.

The other major uncles were Mike, Barry and Dave, in that order.

Mike lasted for six months or so, from when I was eight. He was an actor too, but I didn't like him very much.

He was nothing like Joey. He wasn't any fun at all, and I could tell that he didn't really like having me around. He always wanted to take Mother out without me, and although he had a car, he never wanted to go anywhere exciting in it, like the seaside or fairgrounds. Joey loved fairs as much as I do. One night he took Mother and me to the fair on Hampstead Heath and we went on the big wheel so many times that I was sick all over the place. That *was* a lovely evening. I've still got the plaster black panther with red jewelled eyes that I won on the darts.

Actually, there isn't much more to tell you about Mike except that he stopped coming too, and I breathed a sigh of relief. Mother didn't seem to mind much either, in fact she seemed quite jolly – not like the months after Joey stopped coming. I think *she* really liked Joey too.

Barry appeared at my tenth birthday party, of all places. His son James was in my class at school. James wasn't a friend of mine, so I was quite surprised when Mother insisted that I invited him to the party, especially as all my friends were girls. I was even more surprised when his father (Barry) brought him, and it turned out that James was motherless in the same way as I'm fatherless.

Anyway, as I expect you've guessed by now, Barry and Mother got together. I suppose they must have thought it a great chance to have a ready-made family. Barry had a car, and James and I got really fed up, being forced to play with each other every weekend. Our poor parents! They did try so hard with us and with each other.

There was one awful Sunday when we all went to the seaside. It was a dreadful day, very cold and windy, with ink-coloured clouds spitting rain. We all huddled on the beach wearing plastic macs and anoraks, with the sea pounding furiously on the sand and no one else in sight. James and I went for a race down the beach, mainly because we were freezing to death, but also because we thought the parents might like to be on their own for a while. We found a place in the sand-dunes where the howling wind swept over the top, leaving us a sheltered nook to huddle in.

James was smaller than me (mind you, so is just about everyone else, I'm obviously going to be a giant as well as all my other disadvantages). He was an athletic kind of boy, only interested in football and that sort of thing. He never wanted to chat or draw pictures, so the only activities we had in common were swimming, and sitting together in the back of the car when the parents were taking us somewhere. Sometimes we had fights as well. We once had a dreadful fight in the back of the car when they had to stop and drag us off each other. James had been tickling me, and I *kept* asking him not to, but he just wouldn't stop and in the end I flew at him. He pulled out a huge tuft of my hair and I bit his hand. Barry and Mother said they were ashamed of us.

18

Anyway, there we were, James and I, in a sand-dune digging a hole.

"I wish you were a boy," he announced suddenly, sitting back on his heels and staring at me in that nasty way he had.

"Well *I* wish you were a *girl*," I snapped in reply.

"Oh don't be so stupid," he said. "I wasn't getting at you. I really *do* think it might be easier if you were a boy. We might get on better."

"Or we might get on better if you were a girl," I said. "Girls are better than boys *anyway*."

James ignored my remark. "Do you think they're in love?" he asked, looking at me very intensely. His nose was bright red with cold. I considered the matter.

'No," I replied. "I think they'd like to be though. I think they'd *like* to get married so we could have parents."

"Where would we live?" asked James. "Your flat's too small and gloomy. I suppose you'd have to come and live with me and my dad. We've got a house *and* a garden so there's more room."

"There's nothing wrong with our flat," I snarled. "It's lovely, and I wouldn't come and live in your rotten house anyway and neither would my mother, *and* she wouldn't want to marry your fat old dad. She's too beautiful for him anyway."

And then I did something even more horrible than all the spiteful things I'd just said. I picked up a handful of sand and threw it right into James' eyes, and while he was blinded I hurled myself on top of him and started punching him as hard as I could. The grown-ups were too far away to hear the shrieks and screams, so the fight went on for ages.

"*Anyway!*" bellowed James, pinning my arms with

his knees and twisting my ears almost completely off my head. "You haven't even *got* a real father *anyway*. At least *my* mother comes to visit me once a month!"

"So what then?" I screeched back. "So why doesn't she live with you then Mr Clever Clogs? *My* dad's a prince in another country and he's going to come and fetch me one day soon, *and* my mother, so *there*!"

It was the worst fight I've ever had in my whole life and it went on until the bitter end and we lay exhausted in the cold sand. My ears were scarlet and twice their normal size and my lower lip was sticking out like a duck's bill. James' cheek had five deep furrows where I had raked his face with the remains of my fingernails and his eyes were terribly bloodshot from the sand. Added to which, James didn't have any buttons left on his coat, and the hood of my anorak was torn off.

The parents were appalled at the state of us when we came limping up the beach, each accusing the other of starting it. On the way home I refused to get in the back of the car with James, and Mother gave me one of her rare clips round the ear and ordered me to get in or else. So I did.

That was more or less the end of Barry and James. I felt awful about it as I knew it was me who'd messed it up for everyone, although I didn't think Mother was nuts about Barry or anything. Anyway, I tried my best to apologize to Mother, but she wouldn't talk about it.

She never will talk about her men. She gets furious if I lure her into chatting about them. I think it's because she wants me to have a Proper Childhood, with walks and flowers and trips-to-the-museum, and Nothing Sordid for me to worry my little head about.

There wasn't anyone else for ages after Barry and

James. It was a bit awkward at school because, as I've mentioned, James was in my class and he used to get his friends to gang up on me – not that I cared. I have an invisible magic shield and things like that just bounce off me (well, most of the time).

About six months ago, Dave appeared. He's a jewellery designer, and Mother met him at a party given by Martin and Ruth at the shop. I quite like him actually. He made Mother a lovely pair of gold ear-rings shaped like birds.

He's *brilliant* at drawing, and sometimes he sends me little pictures, and letters with drawings on through the post. A few weeks ago, he sent me one with rainbow-coloured writing on the envelope.

He's absolutely nuts about Mother, and sits around mooning over her and drawing portraits of her all the time. He drew one of me too, but I'm sure it was only because Mother asked him to. No one in their right mind could possibly want to sit and look at *me* for three hours!

He hasn't got a car, but anyway I'm too old to be dragged about with them all the time now, thank goodness. They even go out for the evening sometimes and leave me at home, though I can see that Mother doesn't really like to. I have to practically push her out of the door, then when she's gone I feel miserable and wish she'd come back.

I feel sad about Dave really. He's *so* nice, he's crazy about Mother, he's very kind to me, and I think Mother quite likes him too, but I just can't be bothered with it all, I don't know why.

Do you know, only two weeks after he met Mother he announced that he wanted to buy me a bicycle! Of course I'd love to have a bicycle, but I told Mother that

I didn't think Dave *ought* to buy me one as he was probably only doing it to please her, not because he really wanted to. To my surprise, Mother collapsed in fits of laughter over the kitchen table and said that she must have raised some sort of saint.

"Honestly, Susie," she snorted, "I think he'd like to get one for you. He actually does like you, darling. People do you know, not just your adoring mum!" And she flung her arms around me and held me very tightly.

It's odd, but I get really embarrassed these days when Mother goes all sloppy about me. I still like to lollop against her when we're sitting reading or something, but I can't stand being grabbed and cuddled any more, especially in front of people. We used to hold hands everywhere, but I nearly die if she takes my hand in the street now. Linking arms is all right because it's comfy and less childish.

Another thing is now that I'm older, everyone we meet gasps in amazement that anyone so young-looking as Mother could possibly have such a decrepit-looking daughter as me. Then they all start on about what a *gorgeous* little girl I used to be, and who would have guessed that I'd have turned out so...er... well...tall.

By the way, before I forget, I didn't let Dave buy me the bike. Zöe says I must be a raving lunatic.

I wish I didn't feel so sorry for Dave. He's so nice to me but I just can't bring myself to be terribly nice back. I'm not horrible to him or anything, I just feel sort of frosty whenever he's around.

I remember one evening when I'd picked a spray of honeysuckle on the way home, to give to Mother. Dave was there when I let myself in, so I broke the spray of flowers in two and gave them half each. Well, it seemed a bit mean just to give it to Mother.

Anyway, they both looked dreadfully grateful – Mother grateful that I was being nice to Dave, and Dave grateful because he thought I'd finally started to be really friendly.

I wasn't though. I like him, but I don't want him to start getting all over-enthusiastic, and flinging his arms round me, and including me in all their outings together. I'd rather they just did it all without me.

CHAPTER FIVE

I've just looked through the last chapter, and noticed two things. One is that I sounded jealous of Mother having men friends, and it really isn't like that at all. I do hope you believe me. I even like them if they're nice. I just don't want to be in on it, that's all.

Several pages ago, I was (at last!) embarking on the actual story, when I broke off to describe the "uncles". Do you remember? Mother and I were on our way to have lunch at The Harlequin on the Saturday before Father's Day.

On this occasion, Mother tucked her arm into mine as we threaded our way through the Saturday crowds of people all out doing their shopping.

"We must get you a new coat, darling," said Mother. "We can have a look this afternoon if you like. I really think that anorak's had it. Why don't we get you a proper jacket this time? Anoraks are so shapeless."

"Zöe's got an anorak," I replied.

Mother laughed. "Oh, you and Zöe," she said. "Here we are."

She held open the door of The Harlequin and we went inside. The place was packed, but there were two seats by the window opposite a pair of old ladies.

The Harlequin is a sort of cross between a café and a restaurant. There are booths round the walls and windows, and circular tables with chairs in the middle of the floor. We always try to get a booth because the seats are padded and it's more private. Waitresses come and take your order and there are appalling framed paintings all over the walls, showing lakes and valleys and hideous little boys with tears rolling down their cheeks. I don't like to boast, but some of my paintings are better than those.

Mother and I shuffled into our booth and the old ladies shuffled their legs and moved their shopping bags so we wouldn't all bash knees. They were having a loud conversation about buses. In fact I think they were both deaf as they seemed to be shouting into each other's faces. Mother and I exchanged glances, and I could see that it would take a lot of control on both our parts not to burst into giggles. Mother's as bad as me when she gets going.

"No manners at all!" shrieked the old lady on our left, who was wearing one of those velvet hats that look like brains. "I was at that bus-stop, you know, the one in Lattimer Street, for half an hour, *and* I was first in the queue, and all those louts from that dreadful school up the road came swarming round the bus-stop, and when the bus came (four at once *as* usual and all of them full) they just trampled me in the rush to get on; and then when I finally limped on to the bus, there was nowhere to sit down and not one of them stood up for me, *not one*! *I* told them though. *I* told them what I thought of them. 'No manners,' I said. 'No respect for anyone, you little hooligans.'"

Mother and I buried ourselves in the menu as the conversation zoomed on over our heads like fighter planes.

"What are you having, Susie?" asked Mother. This was another joke, as we always have the same thing.

"Well," I mused, "I think I'll have ... er, sausages, beans and chips and a Coca-Cola. How about you?"

"Well," said Mother, "I might just try the ham salad

25

followed by a glass of milk."

We laughed. We laugh rather a lot actually. We have a very similar sense of humour.

The waitress came and took our order. Her name is Doris, and we know her quite well as we've been coming here every Saturday now for years. I hope she never leaves. She's small and granny-like and she always calls me her little girl. She doesn't seem to have noticed that I've grown about four feet since she first saw me.

"How's my little girl today?" she says. "Same as usual is it? Sausages for my little girl and salad for Mum?"

When Doris had gone off to the kitchen, Mother and I couldn't think of anything much to say. This was partly because it was a bit difficult to concentrate, with the two ladies bellowing at each other only a couple of inches away.

"Nice time with Zöe today?" Mother asked, brightly.

"Mmm," I replied.

"Seeing her tomorrow?" said Mother.

"No," I answered. "It's Father's Day tomorrow and she's got to stay at home."

Then I suddenly got dreadfully embarrassed. I started to go red up the back of my neck, and felt so hot that I had to struggle out of my anorak. After I'd done that, I began madly stirring up the sugar with the sugar spoon.

"What on earth's the matter, Susie?" asked Mother looking right into my face, which only made matters worse. "You've gone bright red . . . you haven't been *up* to anything have you?"

I didn't answer.

26

"Then there's that *nasty* little boy in the flat up-stairs," bawled the old lady in the brains-hat. "Leaves his — what do they call those dreadful things? — roller skates, that's it! Leaves his roller skates on the stairs every day. I *tell* him. Every day I tell him, 'You could break someone's neck leaving those contraptions lying around!' That's what I say to him, but *he* doesn't care. None of them do these days, that's the trouble. Do you know, he even sticks out his tongue at me, and the *language*! You wouldn't believe what he called me yesterday. What are their mothers teaching them? That's what *I'd* like to know."

Doris brought the lunches, and I busied myself with cutting up the sausages and squirting tomato sauce all over everything. Then I couldn't eat it and, even worse, my eyes filled up with tears. A tear splashed on my baked beans, then another and I just couldn't make them stop, so I buried my face in my hands and prayed that no one would say anything. I would have rushed out, but I was trapped on the inside of the booth.

The old ladies had stopped shouting, and I knew they must be staring at me. An arm slid round my shoulders and Mother's voice at its softest whispered, "What is it, darling?" She sounded almost frightened. I hadn't cried for ages and she knows how I hate scenes, so she must have been racking her brains for some truly awful explanation.

"Susie," she whispered again, her hand tightening on my shoulder. "What *is* it?"

"Feeling poorly is she?" shouted the old lady in the brains-hat. "Looks pale to me, doesn't she, Bett? I thought she was looking peaky when she came in. Make her put her head between her knees in case she feels faint."

27

"Can we go please?" I pleaded from between my fingers.

"Of course," said Mother.

Then there was much bundling into my anorak and bustling out of the booth, and Mother paying for the uneaten food, and people looking at me, and Doris patting me, until finally we almost fell out of the door into the bright, busy street.

I still couldn't stop crying (though I couldn't think why) but fortunately everyone in the street was too busy rushing in and out of shops to notice us.

"Come on," said Mother, grabbing my arm.

She steered me away from the main road and through the side-streets, till we came to a little public garden with flower beds, two green benches (both empty) and pigeons grubbing round the litter bins.

"Now then, what is it?" she asked, sitting me down firmly on a bench and looking intently into my face.

I thought about it for a few moments, but I really had no idea what had upset me. Also, I suddenly had the mad desire to start laughing.

"I don't know," I said. "I really *don't* know."

"Well there must be *some* reason, Susan," she said, sounding slightly annoyed. "We've just left two perfectly good plates of food in that restaurant because you were in such a state. What were you thinking about before you got upset?"

I sat and looked at the pigeons, wondering if I was going to snort with laughter, or start crying again.

"*I* know what it was," said Mother, suddenly. "It was Father's Day, wasn't it? You mentioned Zöe and Father's Day and then you went all funny. *Was* it that?"

"It might have been," I replied. "But I honestly don't

know. I'm ever so sorry about our food, Mummy, really I am. I didn't mean to cry, I just couldn't help it."

Mother smiled at me. "You haven't called me Mummy for ages," she said. "Oh Susie, *was* it Father's Day? Do you really mind not having a father? We've always been all right, haven't we? You must tell me if there are things you want that I don't give you. Most children hardly ever see their fathers anyway, they're usually out at work all the time."

"Zöe's dad isn't," I answered. "*He's* nice, and he does shifts and he's often home in the afternoons."

"Well," said Mother, "they're not all like Zöe's dad." And to my surprise, her grey-cloud eyes filled up with tears as if with rain.

Then she tossed her head and laughed. "What a pair of old miseries we are!" she exclaimed gaily. "Sitting here making each other gloomy. Let's go and look at the puppies in the pet-shop window. Do you remember how we used to choose one each and pretend to take them home with us on leads?"

She pulled me to my feet, and we went to the pet-shop to see the puppies. There weren't any that day, but there was a tumble of kittens pressed up against the glass fast asleep. I think kittens are very pretty, but I've never wanted one the way I've wanted a dog. I don't think a cat would need you in the same way as a dog.

On the way home, I kept thinking how Mother had said "They're not all like Zöe's dad," in that dark, mysterious way. It was the only clue she had ever given me about my own father, and I wondered what had happened between him and Mother to make her so sad all those years later.

CHAPTER SIX

Dave turned up later in the afternoon, but I heard Mother at the front door saying she'd like to be alone with me for the rest of the day. Then they started speaking in low voices and I heard him go off down the steps.

Mother was very sweet to me that evening. We sat on the sofa in our dressing-gowns and read our library books, with a tape on the cassette player. I love those sort of evenings, just the two of us, reading quietly and humming along with the tape.

After a while, she put down her book and started sewing one of my sheets which I'd put my foot through the night before.

I plucked up all my courage and suddenly blurted out, "*Please* won't you tell me about Father?" She stopped sewing and put the sheet down on her lap.

Now I've done it, I thought. But, to my great relief, she wasn't cross at all.

"All right, Susan," she said. "I will tell you. It's obviously been worrying you, and perhaps I have been stupid to make such a secret of it all. I just hoped that you'd never think about him if he was never discussed, and I can see that it was silly of me. I will tell you, but you must promise not to keep asking about it, all right?"

I nodded. I could hardly believe she was actually going to tell me.

"It was like this," she said. "I met your father at drama school and we . . . well, we fell madly in love really. I just thought he was the most wonderful person

I'd ever met. He *was* the most wonderful person I'd ever met!

"He was kind and good fun, oh and very good-looking ... not handsome exactly, but very, very attractive, and of course he was a superb actor. I couldn't believe it when he felt the same way about me too. We spent all our time together, and everything fell into place when we both won the awards for the best actor and the best actress at the college.

"A while after that we both left and got married. I was twenty-one and your father was thirty. He'd done lots of things before becoming an actor. He'd been a zoo keeper of all things for three years. He used to look after the lions and tigers —" she saw my face light up — "yes, I thought you'd like that. Now what were the other things he'd done? Oh yes, he was a travelling salesman for a time, and a swimming-bath attendant.

"Then we had you, and we were so happy at first that I used to wake up singing each morning, but it was round about then that our luck seemed to run out.

"For some unknown reason your father didn't get any work. Nothing turned up, despite his best actor award, not even a commercial on TV and of course I couldn't work because you were a tiny baby. So there we were with hardly any money, and your father started to stay in bed all day and, much worse, when he finally hauled himself out of bed he went out and spent what little money we had getting drunk.

"It was an awful time after such tremendous happiness. In fact I can hardly bear to talk about it even now, he was so miserable and bad tempered. Anyway, I really *don't* want to go into all the ins and outs, but he just got more drunken and despairing as the days

31

went by and it was all very depressing.

"Then one afternoon, he came staggering home from the pub in the worst state I'd ever seen him in. You were toddling about in the living room and I'd just put some tea things on the table. He started picking things up and throwing them round the room, and he grabbed the teapot, which was full of boiling hot tea, and threw it so it missed your head by inches. Actually, to be fair, he obviously hadn't seen you, but that was quite enough for me. I picked you up and fled.

"I left all our belongings there and we stayed at Maria's flat, then I looked around and found this place and we've lived here ever since. And that's all there is really." (Maria is an old friend of Mother's from drama school. She's my godmother and we see quite a lot of her.)

"Do I look like him?" I asked.

"Yes," said Mother. "Exactly like him except for the eyes. His are green, like a cat's, yours are more like mine."

"Do you hate him?" I asked. "Didn't he try to find you?"

"No, I don't hate him," she replied. "He couldn't help falling to bits the way he did. I felt very upset but I didn't hate him. Yes he did try to find me. He sent letters through Maria, and I even met him once or twice at her flat to talk things over, but I'd made up my mind. He was obviously still drinking a lot and I felt so worn out with misery and looking after you that I felt it would be better to forget him and start again. I think it was the teapot incident that was the last straw, really."

"And what does he do now?" I asked, getting interested.

"Right, darling!" said Mother, jumping up. "It's bedtime now. I've told you about him, and you *did* promise not to keep asking me about it. I've already had four questions in the last five minutes and there isn't really anything left to tell you."

I can always tell when it's useless to argue with Mother. She gets this bright and breezy look on her face and starts bustling about. She swept me into the bedroom and shooed me into bed.

"You still look such a baby in your nightie," Mother said fondly, as she stood in the doorway. "Good-night now, and no more worries. All the angels guard you."

"All the angels guard you," I repeated.

She went out and closed the door.

"All the angels guard you" is the end of a little prayer we used to say when I was a kid. We don't say it any more, but it's another odd little custom that we share. Even when I'm grown up and married with children of my own, I expect I shall still mumble "all the angels guard you" before I fall asleep.

CHAPTER SEVEN

I woke up the next morning with a strange, excited feeling. You know how you feel when you shake off the woolliness of sleep, and you remember that something nice, or thrilling is going to happen. Usually it's a birthday or some sort of treat, but I knew there wasn't anything like that, not even seeing Zöe. Then I remembered the conversation with Mother and I realized that a plan was weaving itself together in the back of my mind.

Telling this story is getting more and more difficult! I don't think I'll ever get it finished at this rate. Now I'll have to tell you about Mother's friend Maria before I can get on to the next bit, which is all about me going to pay her a visit.

Also, I haven't even mentioned my grandma (Gramps died when I was six) or Aunt Primrose, Mother's younger sister who used to live by herself on a farm in Scotland. It was ten miles from the nearest village and Zöe and I went to stay with her once for the summer, but that most definitely *is* another story, or this book will be five feet thick by the time I reach the end!

Back to the story. It was the morning after Mother had told me about Father. I could tell that it was still very early because the birds were all singing in that deafening early-morning way, and there were no noises from the street.

I propped myself up in bed and read for a while. Then I sneaked out of bed and made some breakfast for Mother. It was cornflakes, toast with marmalade, and tea. I knocked at her door and heard her grunt, "Come in."

She was right down under the bedclothes; she always sleeps like that, and wakes up very grumpy with her face all cross and crumpled.

"Breakfast!" I announced cheerily. "Sit up before the tea gets cold."

She hauled herself up on to one elbow and bundled the pillows into a heap behind her back. Then she sank back, her eyes screwed up into slits, and stretched her arms out for the tray.

"Bless you, darling," she said. "I don't know how I ever managed a child as lovely as you. You must be a changeling."

"Do you really think so?" I asked eagerly. The idea really appealed to me.

"Definitely," said Mother. "Like the changeling in *A Midsummer Night's Dream*. Aren't you having any breakfast?"

"No," I replied. "I thought I might go on a diet. Do you think my face might get any thinner if I went on a diet?"

"What on earth for?" exclaimed Mother. "There's nothing wrong with your face, darling, it's a lovely shape."

"It's fat," I persisted.

"That's nonsense," said Mother. "Really, Susan, what an idiotic notion. There isn't an ounce of fat on you anywhere. You must have something to eat. Now off you go and fetch a bowl of cereal or I shall go and get it for you myself and then I shan't enjoy my breakfast in bed."

Mother knows how to get round me. I went and prepared a tiny amount of cornflakes and came back

35

and perched on the side of her bed. The plan was beginning to take shape.

"I thought I might go and see Maria this morning," I said casually.

Mother looked interested. "That's a good idea," she said. "I might come along too. I haven't seen her for weeks."

"OK," I said. "But actually, I sort of wanted to see her by myself."

Mother looked a bit hurt, but she covered it up very quickly. "That's all right, darling," she said brightly. "I'll invite Dave over for the afternoon if he's not busy."

"He won't be if there's a chance of seeing you," I said.

"Flatterer!" laughed Mother. "You're *up* to something, Susan Hunter. I know you, and there's something decidedly odd going on. Still, as long as it doesn't involve robbing banks then I shall turn a blind eye to whatever it is."

"I think I'll be off then," I said.

"Not at this time of the morning," said Mother. "Maria won't be up for ages yet. It was her last night in that play yesterday and there would have been a party afterwards, so she wouldn't have got to bed until at least three o'clock in the morning. I shouldn't think she'd be too delighted if you went bouncing round there at the crack of dawn. *Tell* you what! Why don't we go up on the Heath together and then you can go along to Maria's later in the morning."

"Would you mind awfully if I went to the Heath by myself?" I asked, feeling very mean.

But Mother insisted that she didn't mind at all and that she had lots to do anyway. She's like that. She

36

never interferes with what I'm doing, not that I often do things I can't tell her about.

The sky had that lovely misty look with no clouds which often heralds a really hot day, so I didn't bother with a coat. I kissed Mother goodbye and dived off down the steps.

It seemed funny going to the Heath without Zöe. We go out together nearly every Sunday morning, but anyway I had decided that this was to be my own personal adventure, and no one else was to be included . . . at least at the beginning.

There were lots of people out on the Heath even though it was so early. I whistled for Loki and together we took our secret path which leads to a deep tangle of bushes where Zöe and I have burrowed out a small hollow which we call The Cave. There is only just enough room for Zöe and me to squash inside.

Inside, there is an old bit of rush matting on the floor, which we found in a rubbish skip on the way to the Heath one Sunday morning. We've decorated the walls with an out of date calendar which has a nice picture of a mare and foal, and an old shaving mirror with a crack down the centre which makes your face look all up one side and down the other. Actually, the walls aren't exactly proper walls. We've woven the branches and twigs together, but they still look very rough. In one corner we have buried a box containing modern-day things like a tin-opener, bus and train tickets, a coin, a bath plug, a torch with batteries and a photo-booth photo of Zöe and me pulling revolting faces. It's for people to find in thousands of years' time, like the people who dig up Roman remains nowadays.

On this particular day I crawled into the gloomy hollow of leaves and branches.

"It is I, Susan," I announced, peering into the mirror. "Susan, guardian of The Cave. I come to ask you to bear witness at the start of my Quest."

This must sound absolutely barmy to you, but it is a ceremony that Zöe and I always go through whenever we enter The Cave. Usually we just lay a bunch of wild flowers on the mat. After all, it is a special place, and it seems right to treat it with respect though I can see it looks a bit daft to an outsider.

The Quest was this: I had decided to find out who my father was and get to see him. I wasn't quite sure what I would do when I did see him, but at that point I just wanted to know who he was and take a good look at him.

I took a matchbox out of my pocket and opened it. Inside was a specially prepared piece of paper which looked completely blank but which I had written on in invisible ink. It said: *Susan Hunter, Quest for Father*, the date and my signature.

The matchbox was already sealed with sticky tape and I thrust it deep into the wall.

"When the Quest is ended," I announced solemnly, "I will burn this box and peace will be mine again."

I crawled out on my hands and knees, stopping to listen before I reached the path. No one was there so I slithered out and brushed the leaves and dust off me.

It was a lovely morning as I had expected, with a strong wind rustling all the trees and bushes so they sounded like the sea. I ran all the way to the edge of the heath, imagining Loki bounding along beside me barking for joy.

CHAPTER EIGHT

The next stage in the Quest was to go to Maria's flat. I had to take a bus to get there, so I sat at the front on the top deck where I could watch the world passing by. When I was a kid, I used to hold the rail and pretend I was driving the bus. It's years since I've done that now.

I'd better tell you about Maria before I launch off into something else! Maria lives by herself in a tiny bed-sitting room, with a tiny kitchen through a door on one side and an even tinier bathroom through a door on the other. Fortunately Maria is tiny too, even smaller than Mother. She has her hair cut short in that urchin style, and you never know what colour it's going to be because she's always dyeing it. It's been black, orange, blonde and silvery but it always looks nice whatever colour it is. She is absolutely bouncing with energy and always seems to be in a good mood. She was Mother's best friend at drama school and they still see a lot of each other.

Maria has marvellous parties and I'm always invited along with Mother. I used to love going when I was little, but nowadays I feel so shy when there are lots of people around that I'd really rather not go.

Maria once had a party where we all had to dress up as clowns. I was the only child there and all the grown-ups treated me like a princess. Mother and I spent days making our suits out of old jumble-sale material, at least, Mother did the making. I just hung about being a nuisance. We even had red ping-pong balls on elastic for our noses. Mother is the only person I know who can look beautiful with a ping-pong ball on the end of her nose! I've got a polaroid photo of us in costume somewhere. It was in the days when I still had blonde curls and the nose hadn't blossomed forth – it's such a pity I had a ping-pong ball stuck over it.

Maria's done quite well at acting. She's just finished a play in the West End of London. That's where all the important theatres are. It was only a small part, but the play ran for a long time.

One thing I've noticed about actors and actresses is that they're always worried about money because they're never sure how long a play is going to last.

The play Maria was in ran for eight months – oh, and I've just remembered she's in that advert for crisps on the TV. You must have seen it, the one where all the crisps shower out of a giant packet and the lady opens her umbrella and dances about while the crisps all bounce off and pile up round her. Well, that's Maria. I've only seen it twice because we don't have a TV, Mother doesn't believe in it. She says we wouldn't do anything at all if we had one, and sometimes, when I see Zöe and her lot all glued to it for hours on end I can see what she means. On the other hand, you can't drag me away once I get near a television set, and I love cartoons, even the ones in adverts. In fact I must admit that I *would* quite like to have a TV really. You feel so left out at school when everyone's going on about some new programme.

Anyway, I realized that Maria must have known my father very well if they were all at drama school together, so I decided to try and wheedle as much information out of her as possible. I felt a bit guilty because I would have to pretend I knew more than I did, otherwise she wouldn't tell me anything, particularly after years of not mentioning him at all.

I rang the bell and Maria's voice crackled over the intercom.

"Who is it?"

"Susan!" I shouted.

"Susan?" asked the sleepy voice.

"Your fairy godchild!" I bellowed.

"Susan!" shrieked Maria, sounding delighted (good old Maria, she's always so pleased to see me).

"Come on up."

The buzzer sounded and the door swung magically open. I sometimes pretend that I've commanded it to open with my magic powers.

Maria opened the door of her room. Her hair was brilliant green with a red tuft at the front, and she was wrapped in a purple satin dressing-gown. I had never seen her hair looking quite so amazing and I couldn't help letting out a gasp. It looked as if there was a parrot sitting on her head!

Maria laughed and ran a hand over the astonishing mane. "I had it done for the party," she explained. "It does look a bit mad, doesn't it? I nearly died of fright when I saw it in the mirror just now. Anyway, it's good to see you, Susie. Come on in."

She flung an arm round me and ushered me into the room. I don't know if it's because I'm getting bigger, but the flat looks more miniscule every time I see it.

"What time is it? Eleven o'clock," she asked and answered herself, looking at her watch. "Oh well, time I should be up anyway. Come on, let's have a coffee. Sit down if you can find a space."

She let the blind up with a bang, and sunlight streamed into the room.

It was difficult to know where to sit. Clothes were

41

festooned all over the chairs, bed and floor, and the rest of the room was bursting with books, magazines, old newspapers and used coffee cups on every available surface.

There were photos all over the walls, showing the plays and shows that Maria had been in, and a poster-sized one of her in that crisp advert I was telling you about.

"Sorry about the mess, darling!" called Maria, as she clattered about in the kitchen washing up cups and putting the kettle on. "We had a party till nearly five in the morning, and I didn't get home till six. You'll have to forgive the squalor, I'm going to have a grand tidy today. It's lovely and sunny, isn't it?"

She brought the coffee in and curled up on the bed. I had cleared a space on a bean-bag chair which was knee-deep in coats and newspapers, and Maria handed me my coffee which I put on the floor. I hate coffee, but I felt too shy to ask for anything else.

"Well now, Susie," said Maria. "What brings you here to see me, or is it just a passing visit?"

"Not exactly," I said, taking a deep breath. "It's Mother. She's told me about Father."

Maria's eyebrows shot up and her eyes danced with excitement. "She *hasn't!*" she exclaimed.

"She *has*," I asserted. "Yesterday."

"*Well!*" said Maria, letting her breath out in a long, astonished sigh. "I don't believe it. That's amazing, and after all this time too. You know she made me promise never to tell you anything about him at all."

"It is strange, isn't it," I agreed. "Perhaps she thought I ought to know about it now that I'm older."

I couldn't think how to ask Maria for more information, without revealing that I didn't know who he

42

was. Then Maria took a sip of coffee and said, "How do you feel about having such a famous daddy then?"

FAMOUS! The word leapt at me in neon lights and whirled around my head. Had I heard properly? Had she really said famous? She had!

"I suppose you've seen him on TV without even knowing who he was," she continued. "It must be very odd for you."

"Oh yes," I gasped. "Very odd — I mean, no! I haven't seen him. We haven't got a TV."

"So you haven't," said Maria. "Pet doesn't like the television, does she? It's not *just* that she thinks it's bad to have one — she had one when you were tiny. It's my guess that she couldn't bear to see Lloyd on the screen every week. She was nuts about him, you know. I sometimes still think she is in a weird sort of way although she never talks about him."

LLOYD! The name joined the word FAMOUS whirling round my mind. Lloyd Hunter.

"Was he nice at drama school?" I asked.

"*Nice!*" echoed Maria. "He was wonderful. The entire college was batty about him — me too, but it was your mama that he fell for. Mind you, she *was* the most beautiful girl in the whole place and always had streams of admirers. Lucky Pet, I used to be so envious of her.

"It was such a terrible shame when Lloyd went to bits and started all that drinking. Your poor ma, with a baby, and no money, and Lloyd getting into drunken rages because no one was offering him any work.

"After they broke up, he was round here all the time pleading with me to get her to change her mind, and I did try. But your mother had decided to devote herself to you and that was absolutely that. Did she tell you about the incident which made up her mind?"

"The teapot," I said.

"That was it," said Maria. "Well you can't really blame her for feeling appalled, but I think she could have given him another chance. He really did seem heartbroken and it was obvious to everyone else that he was devoted to both of you, but she wouldn't hear of it. Then he went off to America, pulled himself together and gave up drinking, and struck lucky as the Stranger in *Worlds Apart* and that's how it all started happening for him.

"I haven't seen him for ten years now, but he's coming back to London in the autumn. Hey, perhaps that's why Pet suddenly told you about him. Perhaps she's hoping to see him again."

"Oh no," I said hastily. "I don't think it's that. In fact, to be truthful, she didn't just tell me, I asked her. And she wasn't too keen on telling me either. I had to wring it all out of her."

"Oh, I see," said Maria, looking disappointed.

"I wonder why he's coming back?" I asked.

"It's because he got fed up being typecast as the Stranger," replied Maria. "He's coming to London to do a new play. It's going on in the West End and I'm sure it'll do well whatever the play's like because all the Stranger fans will come to see it.

"I only know that he's coming back because there was an article about him in the *TV Times* last week. I expect I'll sneak along and see what he's like in it, but don't let your ma know will you? She can't even bear to talk about him to me, her old buddy.

"You know, she was so utterly firm about not having anything to do with him again. I've never seen anyone so single-minded about anything. She wouldn't

44

accept any money from him or let him know where she was living, and she wouldn't let me tell him either.

"He wrote to ask me several times after he'd gone to America, but it was very difficult when Pet wouldn't allow me to tell him anything, and in the end he stopped writing."

I sat in stunned silence. Lloyd Hunter, *my* father, star of *Worlds Apart*, the Stranger! Why, everyone at school went round talking about the Stranger. Zöe even had a poster of him on her bedroom wall which I'd idly sat under, not guessing for one second that he was my own father. It was almost too incredible to believe.

"Do you want to stay and have some lunch?" asked Maria. "I'll have to nip out to the corner shop. It's open till twelve on Sundays. Do you still like sausages, sausages, sausages, or possibly sausages with sausages?"

"I'd love to stay," I said, trying to keep the excited quaver out of my voice, "but I really ought to get home. I've got quite a lot of history homework to finish before tomorrow."

This was true, but I also wanted to get away and think.

Maria showed me to the front door of the house.

"Tell your mother to come and see me soon," she said. "I'm out of work now, so we could go out in the evening sometime."

"All right," I said. "I'll tell her, oh and Maria, please don't mention that I've discussed Father, will you? You know what she's like about private things."

"Cross my heart," said Maria. "I won't breathe a word."

CHAPTER NINE

I went down the road and sat on the low wall next to the bus-stop. I wanted to grab people passing by and tell them, "My father's the star of *Worlds Apart*. He's on telly every week and he's *my* dad!"

Of course my first thought was to dash round to Zöe's house and astonish her with my news, but then I realized that she just simply wouldn't believe me.

For years now, Zöe had patiently listened to my tales of who my mystery father was. He'd been a king, an astronaut, a deep-sea diver, a pop star, even a lion tamer, but for some reason I had never thought of a famous actor, although it was the only one that could have been at all likely. No, Zöe definitely wouldn't believe me.

Then I thought about Mother, and what a strange person she is. I mean, most ladies would give anything to have been married to the star of a big TV programme, but my mother won't even mention the fact to anybody.

I must confess that I began to feel a bit cross when I thought of how poor we'd always been, when we could have lived in a fine house and had everything we wanted. Why, I could have had a horse as well as a dog.

Then I felt guilty, because she'd always been such a nice mother, and even grubbing round the jumble sales had been fun because of her.

Perhaps it wasn't right to want her to do something she didn't want to do. Anyway, he *had* thrown a teapot over my head, even if he was drunk at the time. It's still no excuse, is it? I might have been scalded.

I went home and surprised Mother by working hard at my homework all afternoon. In the evening, Dave called for her and they went out to the pictures. They asked me if I wanted to come, but I politely said that I was going to bed early.

The minute they'd gone, I rang Zöe and asked her when *Worlds Apart* was on. She told me it was on Fridays at seven o'clock, and why on earth did I want to know all of a sudden on a Sunday evening? I told her that everyone in school was talking about it, and I was fed up being the only girl in school who'd never seen it. Zöe said I was weird.

I asked her how Father's Day went, and she told me that they'd all given their dad cards, and taken him breakfast in bed, and the boys had cleaned the car, while she'd just hung around being bored. We said goodbye and I promised to call for her in the morning.

I could hardly wait till Friday when *Worlds Apart* was on TV. On Monday after school, I went round to Zöe's house and spent the whole afternoon gazing at the poster of the Stranger. He was wearing a suit which was a cross between a caveman's furs and a modern spacesuit, but you could see his head clearly. Mother was right, I do look very like him, except for the eyes. He has tousled blondish hair, very wide cheekbones and green cat's eyes. He looks very handsome in a craggy sort of way. I wish it was all right for girls to look craggy.

Zöe got really sick of me looking at the poster.

"*I* know what it is!" she said suddenly. "You've fallen in love, haven't you? You've got a crush on the Stranger."

I snorted with secret laughter.

"No I haven't," I said. "I just happen to *know* something, that's all."

"*Honestly*, Susan Hunter," said Zöe, "you are infuriating sometimes. I am your best friend, aren't I? We *do* tell each other everything at all times, don't we?"

"Yes," I said. "I'm sorry. The thing I just happen to know is that the Stranger is coming to London in a few weeks to be in a play."

"Is that all!" said Zöe with a sneer. "Everyone knows that anyway. It's been in all the papers and there was that article in the *TV Times* last week."

"Oh!" I exclaimed. "Can I see it? Have you still got it?"

"What on earth's the matter with you, Susan?"asked Zöe. "What's this *thing* about the Stranger all of a sudden? You never even want to watch TV unless there's a cartoon on – you *have* got a crush on him, haven't you?"

"No I haven't," I said, crossly. "But I would like to see the *TV Times* if you've still got it. *Please* Zöe."

Zöe went downstairs and reappeared bearing the magazine, which she put on to my lap open at the right page.

I felt aglow with excitement as I saw his picture smiling up at me. We even have similar teeth! The article was only a few lines entitled "No Stranger".

"Lloyd Hunter," it read, "British-born star of *Worlds Apart*, returns to his native soil this summer to start a six-week run of a new play in the West End of London.

"Says 42-year-old Lloyd, 'I get a little tired of being known only as "the Stranger" and would like to get back into "serious" acting for a while. The theatre was always my first love.' However, *Worlds Apart* fans

48

need not worry. A new series has just been completed which will be screened in the autumn, when the present series comes to a close."

"Can I keep this article, Zöe?" I asked.

"Of course," said Zöe. "It's out of date now anyway. You're a nut you know, Susan. Nutty. An N-U-T-case of the first order."

"*I* know," I said, ripping out the article and putting it in my pocket. "Still, it takes one to know one."

Zöe picked up a pillow and threw it at me and we collapsed in giggles and had a mock fight. We never really fight, after all she is my best friend.

Friday arrived, and by seven-thirty I was at Zöe's house, glued to the television. Zöe kept teasing me by saying that her dad would want to watch something else. He didn't though, they're all *Worlds Apart* fans.

It's quite good actually, and I rather enjoyed it, apart from nearly exploding with my amazing secret. The story is about a man from a far-off planet who crashes his spaceship on earth and can't get home. He stays with an ordinary American family who don't know that he's from space, and he has all these magical powers so he's always helping the family without them knowing. He also has a girlfriend pining for him at home on the other planet, as well as a beautiful blonde American lady who he can't marry because of his girlfriend pining at home!

I liked the part about him having magical powers, especially when I thought about my own "magical powers" such as opening Maria's front door, and The Cave, and Loki. I'm also rather good at willing our self-lighting gas cooker to turn on!

When the programme finished, Zöe announced to the entire family that I was in love with the Stranger.

Honestly, I could murder that girl sometimes. Anyway, they all started teasing me so I went off home in a huff.

There were two more months to go until my father arrived in England. It was awful, dragging through each day. Fortunately, the weather really perked up and Zöe and I spent most of our time on the Heath or at the swimming baths when we weren't at school.

July was a bit boring, because we had to work like mad for the end of term tests, and then after we'd broken up for the holidays, Zöe had to go and stay with her gran in the country for two weeks. August was a bit better. Zöe was back, and the weather was even hotter. We both got quite brown from being out of doors so much, at least *I* got brown, Zöe went scarlet and then it peeled off.

Finally, the end of August arrived and so did my father. There was a picture in the newspaper of him arriving at Heathrow airport, in a denim shirt and jeans. The caption read: "The Stranger has landed. Lloyd Hunter, star of the popular American TV series *Worlds Apart*, arrived at Heathrow Airport this afternoon to a rousing welcome from fans of the show. British-born Mr Hunter has not returned to this country for ten years now. 'It's great to be back,' said Mr Hunter, who looked fit and suntanned. 'I'll be interested to look up old friends and see how the country's changed while I've been away.' Mr Hunter will be appearing in *Out of the Depths*, a new play being given its first airing in the West End."

Because Mother used to be an actress, I knew that there would be several weeks' rehearsal before the play began showing to the public.

I wondered if I might sneak along to the rehearsals but they're usually held at a church hall somewhere remote, and with someone as famous as my father in the cast (doesn't that sound funny!), it would be very difficult to find out where it was.

The only thing to do was to be patient and wait till it opened, though even then I knew it would be useless going along for the first few weeks as there would be lots of fans and fuss, and I wouldn't be able to get near him.

Being patient was very difficult, but fortunately there was quite a lot to do, going back to school for one thing, and also my twelfth birthday. Mother took Zöe and me to the pictures as a treat. We saw Walt Disney's *Bambi*. Yes I know, it's babyish, but I really do love cartoons and I hadn't seen that one. The bit where Bambi's mother got shot had the whole cinema in tears (including all the grown-ups) and one little girl of about three got in such a state that her mother had to take her out.

Afterwards, we went to my favourite posh restaurant which we only go to on special occasions because it's so expensive. I had sausages and chips and an ice-cream, followed by a Coca-Cola, and Zöe had a *prawn cocktail* (euk! they look like dead maggots), and spaghettic bolognese with a banana-flavoured milk shake to drink.

It was one of those outings that was absolutely smashing, all of us in the best of moods, and all marching along the streets with our arms linked, when suddenly Zöe said, "Guess what Mrs Hunter!"

"What?" asked Mother, her eyes alight with the happiness of the day.

"Susan's in *love*!" shrieked Zöe to the whole neighbourhood.

I knew what was coming next and, quick as a flash,

51

I grabbed Zöe's arm and propelled her off down the street before she knew what was happening. I half dragged her round the corner down the next road till Mother was left way behind.

"Susie!" I heard her calling. "What are you playing at?"

"Listen, Zöe," I said. "Please, *please* don't say anything about the Stranger to Mother. *Please* don't, just *don't*. Promise me, quick before she catches us up."

"OK," said Zöe. "Of course I won't if it's going to send you stark raving bonkers like this. I won't if it really matters. Why does — ?"

"Thanks," I interrupted as Mother hurried up beside us.

"What was all that about girls?" she asked.

"Oh nothing," I replied feebly.

"*Nothing?*" echoed Mother. "After all *that* performance?"

"Nothing at all," I said, grinning pathetically.

Mother laughed. "*You*," she said, "are getting downright peculiar in your old age."

"I know this," I said, pulling a mad face, glad to get away from Zöe's remark.

They both laughed and we finished the journey home just as jolly as before. I wondered how Mother must feel when she opens the paper and sees Father's picture in it. I wondered if she ever regretted not seeing him any more.

CHAPTER TEN

The opening night arrived. I rushed out and bought a paper the next morning before I went to school.

"That's about the fifth newspaper you've bought in the last three months, Susan," said Mother. "You never *used* to be so interested in the papers."

"Current affairs!" I said, buttering a piece of toast. "They said it's good for us, at school, to know what's going on in the world."

"I think I'd rather *not* know," said Mother, coming over and kissing me on top of the head. "Goodbye, darling. Don't be late now."

She sometimes leaves early for work if Ruth wants help getting the new stock hung up.

The minute she'd gone, I burrowed through the paper to the review page. *Out of the Depths* was very well reviewed. The critic said that the play had a fascinating twist that he wouldn't reveal, and that Lloyd Hunter proved that he certainly had a lot to offer the English stage. I was delighted for him.

"Lloyd Hunter," I said to myself. "Susan Hunter, daughter of Lloyd and Petunia Hunter."

It sounded so grand.

The next step was actually getting to meet him. I decided that the best time would be in about a week. Monday night would be easiest of all, nice and quiet after the weekend.

The play started at 7.45 p.m. but the paper didn't say what time it would finish, so I rang the theatre, and the man said it ended at 10.20 p.m. In that case it would be best to be there by ten, so I could work out how to get in. It had always been very easy at my mother's theatres because I was well known to everyone, but I knew it would be completely different just breezing into a big West End theatre, particularly with a famous actor inside.

The week crawled past. I was so preoccupied with my plotting and planning that I don't remember anything at all, except Mrs Ratner (we call her Ratbags – not in front of her of course!) sending me out for not paying attention.

On Sunday night I lay awake in bed, far too lit up to sleep. I was arranging everything in my head. Mother thought I was going to stay the Monday night at Zöe's but I wasn't really going to. I would come back from the theatre and stay the night at Maria's flat. It would mean bashing on Maria's door in the middle of the night and telling her what I'd been up to, but I couldn't think of any other way of being out by myself so late. I couldn't ask Maria if it was all right to stay with her before Monday, in case she let Mother know.

"Have a nice time with Zöe," said Mother, as I set off to school the next morning. "Don't be a nuisance to Mrs Rawlings, will you? And *do* be helpful with washing up and things, won't you? Mrs Rawlings has enough to do, with those four children to look after."

"Don't worry," I said.

It was the first real, downright lie I'd ever told Mother, and it felt dreadful. It lay like a lead weight over my heart, accompanied by the dull, nagging feeling that she might find out.

School was unbearable. There was a double maths lesson followed by double home economics. We made a stew . . . at least, it was supposed to be a stew. I can't think how I managed it, but mine was pale whitish-grey with lumps of congealed fat floating about in it. I put the whole nauseating mess into a glass jar to take home, but it made me feel sick just to look at it, so I threw it in the bin.

At last, school was over. I arranged to go round to Zöe's till about eight, which is as late as we usually make it on a weekday. Zöe had no idea of my plan, she just thought I'd decided to come round for a few hours, as I often did.

Before I went to Zöe's house, I nipped home and changed out of my school uniform into my best jeans and lacy pink jumper. I'd even whitened my plimsolls. It was the end of September and quite chilly, so I borrowed Mother's green jacket with the red trimmings. The sleeves are a bit too long, but they look nice turned back into cuffs. I knew Mother wouldn't mind, because she likes me to borrow her things.

Pity about the face, I thought as I passed the mirror on my way out.

"*You're* all done up," said Zöe when she opened the door to me.

"No I'm not," I replied. "I just felt like being smart for once, that's all."

We retired to Zöe's bedroom and listened to pop music on her radio. I passed the time by drawing a portrait of her. It was rather a good one and she stuck it up on her wall.

"Time you were off, Susan!" Mrs Rawlings called up the stairs.

"Coming!" I called back.

Zöe saw me to the front door and suddenly I wished desperately that she was coming with me.

"Zöe," I said urgently. "Wish me luck."

"What for?" asked Zöe.

"Never mind why," I said. "I'll be able to tell you soon but not just yet. Wish me luck though, please, you know, the way the Guardians wish each other luck."

"Oh Susan, that's a bit silly," she said. "We don't do that any more."

"*Please*," I said. "No one's looking."

Zöe shrugged her shoulders. "All right," she said, holding out her arms. We clasped each other's wrists.

"The Guardian greets you," said Zöe, "and wishes you all success on this – what is it that I'm wishing you good luck for?"

"Quest," I answered.

"All success on this Quest," replied Zöe. Then we let go of our wrists and pressed our fingertips together.

"Thanks," I said.

"That's all right," mumbled Zöe. "You will tell me soon though, won't you?"

"As soon as I can," I said. "Good night."

I walked backwards down the path waving, until I was out of sight behind the hedge. Then I ran all the way to the underground station.

The clock above the ticket office said 8.15 p.m. I had two hours before the play was over, and I felt a strange mixture of delight and anxiety to be alone in London for the first time, with no one expecting me anywhere.

I bought a ticket to Leicester Square and went down on to the platform. I sat down next to an elderly American lady and her husband who were perched on the nearest bench. I knew they were American because the lady smiled at me and said in a very American accent, "And where are *you* off to at this time of night, young lady?"

I was rather surprised because I'm usually with Mother and they all exclaim how old I look.

"I'm going to meet my father," I replied. (It's true! I thought.)

"Oh," said the lady. "And are you going to see a show? Won't they all have started by now?"

"He's *in* a show," I answered, feeling rather relieved to be able to mention him.

"Why how exciting," said the man, leaning forward and smiling at me. He had very short, silver hair which looked just like an old teddy bear's fur. "Which show is that?"

"It's called *Out of the Depths*," I told them.

"Well whadaya know!" said the lady. "Wayne and I went to see that yesterday, didn't we, Wayne? To tell you the truth, we thought it was a little teeny bit obscure. The acting was very good though, let me see now, there were two ladies in it and of course Lloyd Hunter. Good heavens child! You don't mean to say that Lloyd *Hunter* is your father?"

I nodded.

"Well of *course*!" said the man. "You look just like him, doesn't she, Angela? What a surprise. I didn't even know he was married. Here comes the train, ladies."

The train rattled its way into the station and the doors hissed open.

"Would you like to sit with us?" asked the lady kindly, and I accepted, feeling quite grateful as I had a lot of time to get through and felt a little nervous about being alone.

It was a very noisy train. All the windows were open so we couldn't hear a word each other said and eventually gave up.

It turned out that they were getting off at Leicester Square too, so we went up into the street together.

Everywhere there were cars and lights and people. At the top of the stairs, the American lady turned to me.

"Well," she said. "We're off to Trafalgar Square. Someone told us that it looks so pretty at night, with the fountains all lit up, and old Nelson way up on his column. Your theatre is right here, so we'll say good-bye now."

"Goodbye," I said, and they walked away and vanished instantly into the river of people.

I felt a bit lost without them.

CHAPTER ELEVEN

I was relieved to see that the theatre *was* next to the station. The name of the play was written on a huge hoarding above the doors, and there were large boards showing the reviews and enormous photos of the three actors. Father's picture made me want to float off the ground with — whatever it is when you feel almost hysterical with excitement.

There was a little sandwich bar opposite with no one in it, so I went across and ordered a cheese sandwich and a chocolate milk shake. The man behind the counter said they didn't do milk shake, so I had a Coca-Cola instead.

I was horrified when the bill came to one pound and sixty-five pence. I fished in my pocket and found that I had only one pound and sixty-eight pence altogether. Father would have to lend me the fare home. The first chill of doubt entered my mind. Suppose I couldn't get in to see him — what then?

I sat and munched the sandwich very slowly, taking miniscule bites and chewing as many times as possible. Across the road, Father's photo smiled out at me like a beacon.

The door opened and a man came in. He was dressed in a very old brown coat with the pocket hanging off. His face was seamed with dirt, and his filthy, iron-grey hair hung in greasy lumps over his collar. He appeared to have great difficulty in keeping still for he was weaving about all over the place, and had to hold on to the counter to stop himself lurching over backwards.

"Sandwich, guv!" he shouted in an odd, aggressive way. "Ham! Chicken, makeitachicken, OK?"

The man behind the counter began making up the sandwich. He had very curly black hair and an undone white overall, underneath which he was wearing a string vest. He didn't look at all pleased with the new customer.

"Eat here or take away?" he asked with an Italian accent.

The new customer jerked his head towards the street to indicate that he wanted to take the food away. In doing so, he overbalanced and fell up against the plate glass window. I realized that he must be drunk.

"You gotta the money this time, Duke?" asked the sandwich man. "This isn't a charity shop you know."

"I got money!" shouted the customer (why do drunk people always shout?). "I'm rich. *Rolling* in the stuff."

He fumbled in his trouser pocket and brought out a handful of silver which he slapped on to the counter so forcefully that it all rolled off on to the floor.

"Take it easy now, Duke," said the sandwich man, putting the sandwich into a bag.

Duke was now on his hands and knees, muttering to himself as he crawled about the floor picking up the coins. He reached under my stool for a tenpenny piece then looked up into my face. His eyes were very pale blue with bloodshot whites, and I felt a stab of fear shoot through me as he smiled, showing rotten stumps of teeth.

"'Ello, girlie," he said, pulling himself to his feet and staggering to the counter. "Mario 'ere thinks I can't pay, see? Thinks I'm a dosser, don'tcha Mario, eh? Well, I'll have *you* know, I was a major in the British

army, twennyfive years. Twennyfive years!" he shrieked, waving a filthy finger in the counter man's face.

The counter man took some of the coins and rang
them up on the till. He pressed the rest of the money
into one of Duke's hands and the sandwich into other.

"On your way now, Duke, OK?" he said.

Duke seemed pacified and made for the door. He
didn't see the glass and walked smack into it. Then he
jerked it open and disappeared with a strange, bouncing step into the night crowds.

Mario leaned back against a panoramic view of a
Swiss valley and stared at me. I felt a bit embarrassed,
as I had eaten the sandwich and only had about two
inches of Coca-Cola left. There's a limit to how long
you can make a glass of Coca-Cola last.

"You're a bit young to be out at this time of night,"
he said. "It's not a-nice to be round here this-a-time of
night."

"My father's in the play across the road," I said.
"I'm meeting him afterwards as a surprise. I think I'll
be off now, goodbye."

I swallowed the last mouthful of Coca-Cola and
hurried out.

The clock in the sandwich bar said only nine o'clock.
Another hour to go and the man was right, it *wasn't* a
nice place to be out at that time of night. A few doors
away, Duke had collapsed in a heap of brown-coated
misery in a shop doorway, muttering angrily to himself. Two policemen appeared from an alleyway and
started yanking him to his feet. Duke raved and pro-
tested, but the policemen marched him firmly off down
the street. The chicken sandwich lay scattered outside
the doorway, and people trod it into the pavement as
they passed by.

61

I knew Trafalgar Square could not be far away, so I decided to try and find my nice American friends. I was beginning to feel nervous hanging about in the street, and hoped I could persuade them to wander around with me till it was time to go to the theatre. They would be very easy to recognize because the man was wearing a brightly checked suit, and the lady a pink coat and a white hat.

I set off down the road that they had taken, turned a corner, and there in front of me lay Trafalgar Square looking rather magical in the orangey glow from the streetlights and floodlights.

Nelson was lit up by a searchlight beam from an arched building nearby and the ladies holding fishes in the centre of the two fountains were lit up as well. So was the whole of the National Gallery which runs along one side of the square and there was a lovely glittering globe on top of one of the buildings behind the gallery.

There were quite a lot of people about, considering that it was getting late. A party of noisy young French people, all dressed in identical yellow anoraks and jeans were messing about near one of the fountains. I looked all around for my Americans, but they weren't there. I felt very disappointed.

Near me, one of the four huge lions who guard the base of Nelson's Column gazed out sadly above my head. On impulse, I shinned up the plinth he rested on and sat down with my back against his magnificent chest. His wonderful great paws were stretched out on either side of me, making a little hideaway. The lions weren't floodlit, so I didn't think it likely that I would attract much attention up there.

It felt marvellous, sitting under his fearsome-looking

head. I pretended that he was real and that everyone who went by was amazed at my courage. I stood up and examined his open mouth and nostrils, which were so big that I could put my fist right inside each one. Then I sat down and looked around me.

Big Ben's illuminated clock hung in the dark sky at the end of one of the wide roads. Nine-twenty, it read. Traffic roared past with winking lights, the occasional pigeon fluttered by bewildered by the strong lighting, and two ladies came past having a loud argument in a foreign language.

Suddenly, I began to have the odd feeling that I was being watched. I was quite right too. A police car had pulled up at the kerb a few yards away, and the two policemen inside were staring at me. One of them got out of the car and began walking towards me.

I started feeling decidedly panicky. What on earth would Mother say if I was dragged home in a police car!

The policeman stopped and looked up at me.

"Hello, love," he said casually. "Getting late, isn't it?"

"Yes," I replied weakly.

"Mum and Dad with you are they?" he asked.

I hadn't thought of that!

"Yes they are actually!" I exclaimed. "They're over there." I waved a hand towards a crowd of people who were milling around nearby.

I hate to sound like a goody-goody, but I really don't tell lies, not blatant ones anyway, and it must have been very obvious to the policeman that I wasn't telling the truth.

"Which ones are they?" he said. "Point them out to me."

Panic gripped me and I went all hot and cold. I felt very trapped up on the plinth with my lion's paws like a fence round me.

"Can I jump down?" I asked. "Then I'll take you over to them."

The policeman offered me his shoulder and I jumped on to the ground. Then I ran for it.

Never in all my life have I run as fast as I did that night. I shot across the middle of the square and up the steps three at a time. In the middle of the square I turned and saw the policeman, very red in the face, tearing after me at a horrifying speed. Astonished faces flashed past as I leapt up the steps and across the road just as the lights were changing from red to green.

The cars roared into action behind me as I reached the opposite pavement. I glanced back and saw the policeman dancing about trying to find a gap in the continuous, racing traffic. It was like the Red Sea rolling across and saving the Israelites from the Egyptians!

However, I only had a few seconds before the Red Sea parted again, so I sprinted up a side alley and across another road until I saw my father's theatre looming up in front of me. I decided that it was safest to get inside before anything else happened to me.

CHAPTER TWELVE

I made my way round to the stage door and tried to think of a plausible way of getting in. I decided to say that I was going to see someone who worked in the wardrobe department (which is where the costumes are looked after). There are usually several people working there, and it was just possible that the doorkeeper didn't know all their names. I smoothed my hair and boldly opened the door.

"Can I help you?" asked a stout, middle-aged man, who was sitting in a little booth rather like a station ticket-collector's box.

"No thanks," I said, trying to sound casual. "I'm just on my way up to the wardrobe."

"*Oh* yes?" said the man in a disbelieving way. "And who might you be wanting to see then?"

I couldn't think of any name at all.

"Elsie Bloomer!" I blurted out.

"Elsie Bloomer?" said the man, sounding amused. "Are you quite sure it's Elsie Bloomer that you want? It wouldn't be Mr Hunter you'd be after now would it?"

"Of course not," I said, knowing that it was pretty hopeless. "It's my Auntie Elsie. I'm supposed to go and see her. She's taking me home after the show."

"Here, Rosie!" the man called through an inner door which stood ajar. "This one wants an Elsie Bloomer, wardrobe mistress!"

Rosie, a pretty, red-haired lady, put her head round the door and burst out laughing. "Look, lovie," she said, "you'll have to do better than that. We've had just about every trick in the book with people trying to get in, but Elsie Bloomer! That really beats the lot. You'll just have to wait till after the show and try to get Mr Hunter's autograph when he comes out of the stage door like everyone else. Now off you go."

"What are you doing on your own here anyway?" asked the man in the booth. "This isn't a nice place for a young girl to be hanging about."

"Oh, my mum's just outside," I said reassuringly, and backed out trying to look casual.

There were two phone boxes a few yards from the stage door. I went into one of them and pretended to be phoning someone, so I could think what to do next.

I was absent-mindedly watching the stage door when it opened, and the doorman came out with a middle-aged lady. He took her to the end of the alleyway where he appeared to be giving her directions.

As fast and quietly as possible, I sneaked out of the box and in through the stage door. Nobody was in the booth or the inner room, which had a large notice saying: ABSOLUTELY NO VISITORS WHATSO-EVER IN THE DRESSING-ROOMS. There were two doors leading off the inner room. The one on the right was half open, so I took that one. It led me to a set of grey concrete stairs, at the top of which was a long corridor with lots of doors on either side. One of the doors had "Ladies" written on it, so I hurried inside and locked myself in one of the lavatories.

I think I can honestly say that sitting in that lavatory was one of the most nerve-racking experiences I've ever had, even worse than being chased by the policeman. I must admit though, I was dying to tell Zöe about that. *Me*! Chased by the police. I suddenly had visions of dozens of police cars, sirens wailing, zooming all over London looking for me.

Fortunately the lavatory was a nice clean one with a door and walls that came right down to the floor so no one could possibly see me. I wished I had something to read. It could only have been about a quarter to ten so I had at least thirty-five minutes to sit there! I wished I'd remembered to wear my watch.

Someone came in and washed their hands. I heard the towel clunking round in the machine and footsteps crossing the floor. I rustled my clothes a bit so that whoever it was wouldn't be worried by the complete silence from my cubicle and think I'd fainted and needed help.

Then another person came in and, to my horror, said "Are you in there, Jen?"

"No!" I called, making my voice as adult as possible. (Unfortunately, my voice is rather high-pitched.)

"Sorry," said the voice.

Phew! I thought.

Then the voice said, "Who *is* that? Is it Cathy?"

"No!" I answered, trying to sound annoyed. "It's *me*."

"Oh," said the voice. "Sorry."

No one else came in for ages, thank goodness. Every so often I heard voices in the distance but that was all. I began to feel very cramped, and tried running on the spot to ease my knees.

I was just beginning to wonder if it might be 10.20 p.m. yet, when I heard the door suddenly crash open and two ladies came in talking to each other. They each went into a lavatory on either side of me. When they came out, one of them said, "Hang on a sec, Nance, I just want to wash my hands."

"How do you think it went tonight?" asked the other voice who, I assumed, must be Nance.

"Oh not bad," said the hand-washer. "They were a good audience, weren't they? I don't think *I* was too brilliant though. Did you notice where I cut in on Lloyd's speech in the kitchen scene?"

At the mention of Father's name, I glued my ear to the door. It was quite difficult to hear, what with the cisterns refilling and the splashy washing going on.

"No," said Nance. "You're just too self-critical, that's all. Lloyd's even worse. Tears himself to shreds every night and he always seems marvellous to me."

"Me too," said the unnamed voice. "He's a nice man, isn't he? Dishy too, but he's always on his own. Never accepts *any* invitations anywhere. He's only been out to eat with us all once since the show began. Still, it is difficult for him, isn't it, what with all the fans and everything. Not like us unknowns!"

They both laughed.

"Do you know something odd?" said Nance. "I heard this rumour that he was married years and years ago, *and* he had a kid and it broke him up when his wife took the kid and left him. I wonder if it's true?"

"If it is, she must have been insane!" said the other voice with a whistle. "He seems absolute perfection to me. Kind, considerate, handsome, *rich*, great actor, only drinks orange juice; he's got the lot really, hasn't he? He's too good to be true."

"Perhaps that's it," said Nance. "There must be something wrong with the guy. Still, *I* wouldn't mind the chance to find out."

They both went out laughing.

As soon as their voices died away, I came out as it was obvious from their conservation that the show had finished.

I was fascinated with their chat about my father and

my heart rose with hope that he might actually be pleased to see me. Before, I'd been slightly worried that he might be a bit embarrassed if I just turned up but, unless he had two families, *I* must have been the kid they had mentioned.

CHAPTER THIRTEEN

I crept along the corridor looking at all the doors. I pushed one open, but it was just a store-room. To the left was another flight of steps which led down. The only other way was back where I'd come from so I set off down the stairs. I could hear lots of voices and bustle as I neared the bottom, and two people suddenly came rushing up the stairs wearing coats and chatting to each other.

"Night, darling," one of them said to me as they passed.

"Night," I mumbled in reply.

The very first door I came to at the bottom of the stairs had LLOYD HUNTER written on it in large gold letters. There was also a newspaper photo of Father, stuck up with a bit of sticky tape. Someone had blacked one of his front teeth with a felt pen and drawn an arrow through his head, with a balloon coming out of the mouth saying, "Ooh, the agony!"

I thought I was going to have a heart attack. This was IT. I'd made it. The Quest was over. My pulse began to race so madly that I felt quite weak at the knees and had to put my hand on the doorframe to steady myself.

I could hear raised voices through the door, in fact, it sounded remarkably as if there was an argument going on. Steeling myself, I knocked very softly on the door. Nobody answered, and the voices continued to rise and fall, so I knocked again. Still no one came to the door, so I plucked up all my courage and opened it.

In the split second that I pushed it open, a voice from

inside shouted, "*Don't* give me that old rubbish, Chris. I was *useless*!" and a horrifying sight met my eyes. An enamel coffee-pot was flying through the air towards me.

"Duck!" someone shrieked, and in the nick of time, I hunched down on to the floor. The coffee-pot sailed on over my head and crashed against the passage wall. I stayed in my crouching position feeling half embarrassed and half shocked.

The two men who were inside rushed out and helped me into the room. One of them was my father.

"My God, girl!" he exclaimed in a shaking voice. "Why on earth didn't you knock on the blasted door? That might have killed you."

He sat me down on a bench next to a huge mirror which had light bulbs all round it. There were cards and telegrams stuck into the edges of the frame and I could see my astonished face reflected in the glass.

"Are you all right?" said Father, turning me round and examining the back of Mother's coat. "I'm afraid your coat's got coffee all over it. God, I am sorry, I haven't been in a temper like that for years." He turned to the other man, whom he had called Chris.

"I'm sorry, Chris," he said. "At least I wasn't throwing it *at* you. I didn't know someone would walk through the door at that moment. I just felt so angry with myself. I really did think I was awful on stage tonight."

"But you always do!" said Chris. "That's always been your trouble since the old days, putting yourself down. It's ridiculous, and anyway, I think you could trust the opinion of your old friend here. I mean, I did *write* the damned thing, it does *matter* to me if I have lousy actors in my plays."

71

They went on like this for about five minutes, completely forgetting that I existed which gave me a perfect excuse to watch them both. Chris was small, with longish, brown curly hair and kind brown eyes. He was wearing a grey shirt with jeans and plimsolls. Father was wearing a black and white striped football shirt and jeans. He did look very like me except for his lovely glittering eyes, which were green and cat-like as Mother had said. Chris suddenly nodded in my direction, and Father swivelled round in his chair.

"I'm sorry, darling," he said. (Theatre people often call strangers "darling", it's a sort of custom.) "First of all I nearly kill you, then I forget you're there! Now what did you want? Silly question, it's an autograph, isn't it? How did you get in anyway? Jimmy watches the stage door like a hawk."

"I sneaked in," I said in a tiny voice.

"Well," said Father kindly, "I think you *deserve* an autograph after sneaking in and narrowly avoiding decapitation by coffee-pot!"

He had picked up an old envelope and was starting to write and I still hadn't told him who I was. The words were stuck in my throat.

"Now then, what name is it?" asked Father, then he peered at me quizzically. "Do you know," he continued, "you look exactly like someone I've met, only I can't think who it is. Isn't that odd. I feel as if I've met you before."

I went bright red. I seem to spend half my life bright red at the moment.

"Right then," said Father briskly. "What shall I put? To . . . what's the name then?"

"Susan," I said weakly. "Susan Hunter."

His pen remained poised in mid-air and his bowed

head moved up slowly till he was looking at me.

"Susan Hunter?" he repeated in the same slightly shocked tone of voice as me.

"Mother's name is Petunia," I said. I didn't know what else to say.

"It *can't* be!" said Father. "What does ... do you ...? My God, Chris!" He turned to Chris, who looked just as stunned as he did.

"It *must* be!" continued Father. "You've got her eyes! Susan! Is it really *my* Susan? But of course it is, I can see it is! That's who you reminded me of, it was *me*!" He closed his eyes and groaned. "And I nearly knocked you out with a coffee-pot. Oh no, you don't know how incredible that is, my poor darling. The last time I saw you it was a teapot! God, what an awful father you've got. *Susan!*" he suddenly yelled my name with a shriek of delight, at the same time reaching out and grasping me by the shoulders. "Let me look at you! Oh, I'm just so astonished I can't believe it. And you're twelve now, aren't you? Chris, look at her! Isn't she lovely?"

He turned me round to the mirror and held my face next to his. The likeness was truly remarkable.

"I've got your nose," I said.

"Oh but it's a nice ladies' version," said Father. "And you've got your mother's wonderful eyes. Chris this is just amazing. Susan, I'd like to introduce you to Chris Lawrence. He wrote the play I'm in at the moment, and he knew your mother, and you, till you were one and a half. We must go and celebrate somewhere. Wait a minute! Where's your mother?" His face lit up. "Is she here too?"

"No," I replied. "She doesn't know I'm here actually. Nobody knows I'm here. I didn't even know you were my father until a few months ago, I found out by myself. Mother doesn't know that I know. At least, she knows I know a bit about you, but she doesn't know I know who you are. She'd go insane if she knew I'd come to find you."

"Wait a minute!" said Father. "She never told you who I am? Why that's crazy. Tell me, Susan . . . has she got anyone special around? You know, a boyfriend, or perhaps you've got a new family by now?"

"Oh no," I said gaily. "At least, there's a man called Dave who comes round a lot, but there've been dozens like him ever since I can remember."

I remembered that I had a strip of photos showing Mother and me in one of those photo-booths. I took it out of my jeans pocket and handed it to Father. I look dreadful in all of them and Mother looks dreadful in one where we're pulling hideous faces at each other, but the other three of her are lovely. Father looked at them with the softest expression on his face.

"Oh, Chris," he said, showing them to his friend. "Look at her, will you? She's just the same."

He turned to me. "Hey!" he exclaimed. "I've got something to show you, too. Hang on a minute."

He dashed across the room and rummaged in a small, battered suitcase. "Here," he said. "Just to show that I hadn't forgotten you."

Father also had a strip of photo-booth pictures. To my surprise, they showed him and a small baby who, I realized with delight, was me. He was holding me up so that my face was directly underneath his. I had a fat baby face with wisps of blonde hair, and in the first two photos I was smiling, the third a little worried-looking, and in the fourth I was bursting into tears. Father was laughing in all of them.

74

"Oh Susan," he said, putting his arms round me, "I can't tell you how thrilled I am to have found you again . . . well, for you to have found me. One of my reasons for coming back to England was to try and find you and Petunia. I rather hoped that she might have forgiven me by this time, but if she didn't even tell you who I am then I suppose she can't have done."

"They're going to come and lock us in soon if we don't hurry up," said Chris. "Why don't we go and eat somewhere?"

"Good idea," agreed Father, putting on his coat. "By the way, Susan, I forgot to ask if you're a fan of *Worlds Apart*?"

"Well not *exactly*," I replied. "At least, I am now I know you're in it, but we don't have a TV and I only saw the programme at the same time that I found out about you."

"Who told you about me?" asked Father.

"Maria," I answered. "But she doesn't know that Mother doesn't know . . . oh dear, it's all very complicated. I'm going to stay with Maria tonight and explain everything to her. I've told Mother that I'm staying the night with a schoolfriend of mine."

"But Maria's on holiday," said Father. "I went round to see her this morning – isn't it incredible, Chris, she's still in that tiny flat – and the landlady said she's on holiday for two weeks. Did she know you were coming?"

"No," I said, my heart sinking. "I was going to surprise her."

"Oh," said Father. "That's tricky, isn't it? Still, we can think about that later; right now the problem is getting out of the theatre and into my car. I've got a big hired Rolls Royce hovering about outside, so let's get ourselves into that and decide what to do while we're driving along."

"Would you mind very much if I didn't come?" said Chris. "I think I ought to be getting back home, and I'm sure you two would like a chat by yourselves. Bye, Susan, don't disappear again, will you?"

We said our goodbyes to Chris, and a few minutes after he'd gone, a large man put his head round the door and asked Father if he was ready.

"Ready for what?" I asked, as Father and I followed the man along the labyrinth of corridors.

"It's a bit difficult getting out," explained Father. "Both the stage door and the front of the theatre are besieged by Stranger fans every night. I used to try and sign a few autographs, but they just swarm all over you. I have a few strong guys to help me shoulder my way through the crowds. You just hang on to my arm or you'll be swept away." We arrived at the little room inside the stage door, and I was rather pleased when Jimmy (the doorman) looked startled to see me.

"My daughter, Susan," said Father, introducing me. "Susan, this is Jimmy Barker."

"I'm so sorry, Mr Hunter," stammered Jimmy. "I had no idea . . . she told me she was looking for . . . well you could knock me down with a feather!"

"It's all right, Jim," said Father, smiling. "You could knock me down with a feather too! What's the crowd like tonight?"

"Dreadful," said Jimmy. "Hundreds of 'em."

There were now six burly men waiting just inside the door.

"Ready?" one of them asked.

"Ready when you are," replied Father.

Then everything started happening very quickly.

76

Someone threw open the door and the men hustled us outside forming a circle around us.

The crowd was enormous, and very out of control, despite a handful of policemen trying to keep order. There seemed to be lights flashing on and off, and a sea of arms waved programmes and pens in our faces amid waves of yelling and laughter. We could hardly move, the crowd was so dense, and I felt frightened. Father must have sensed this because he suddenly picked me up and carried me! I felt dreadfully embarrassed, but he's a lot bigger than me, and I certainly felt safer in his arms.

At last a car loomed up in front of us with the door miraculously open, Father hurled us both inside and the car sped away. The shrieking and screaming faded into the ordinary sounds of traffic and car horns.

The inside of the car was like something out of a dream. There was a thick, furry brown carpet on the floor, brown leather seats and smoked brown windows so people couldn't look in. The front was sealed off by a glass partition, and a young man in chauffeur's uniform was driving unconcernedly along. Father must have noticed my awestruck look.

"I know," he said. "*I've* never got used to it either. When your mother and I were together we had nothing at all. Even your baby clothes came from jumble sales."

"They still do sometimes," I said, instantly wishing I hadn't, as it sounded like fishing for money. "At least they used to, but we're all right now."

"Well, we'll have to see to it that you and Pet can share in my riches," continued Father. "I'm so rich now that it's ridiculous. I mean, there's a limit to how many cars and houses you want. I've just bought a house, actually. It's right bang on the edge of Hampstead Heath. It's got carpets, bathrooms, a garden, the Heath on the other side of the garden, dozens of rooms and no one in them, except me and a lady who comes to clean it all every day. Crazy, isn't it?"

"Did you say Hampstead?" I exclaimed. "Mother and I live near there. We can walk to the Heath in twenty minutes if we hurry. Oh that's wonderful! Perhaps we could come and visit you — oh, I forgot, Mother doesn't seem to want to see you."

"That *is* a problem," said Father. "But right now the main problem is where you're going to stay tonight. Look, as it's half past eleven, why don't I drop you off at your house and you go in and pretend that you got fed up staying at your schoolfriend's or something. I think that would be best. Petunia will still be up, won't she? She never used to go to bed till two in the morning. Oh Susan, there are so many things I want to ask you about, but I really am worried about you deceiving your mother, and I think you ought to get on home as quickly as possible."

"I know," I said. "You're right. I'll say that I just felt like coming home, and hope she isn't too cross with me for walking home from Zöe's so late."

I gave Father the address, and he slid open a little panel on the chauffeur's partition and told him where to go.

"When can we meet again?" asked Father. "How about tomorrow afternoon?"

"I'm at school till four," I replied miserably.

"That's annoying," said Father. "I have to be at the theatre at six-thirty and I want a really long natter with you next time. It'll have to be Sunday. I've got two shows on Saturday, and you're at school for the rest of the week."

We arranged to meet on the Heath at two o'clock on Sunday, by my favourite pond. Father said he'd be wearing a brown false beard and a wig. For a second I thought he was joking, then I realized that it was a disguise so he wouldn't be spotted by *Worlds Apart* fans.

The Rolls purred up to the road where Mother and I live. I asked Father if we could stop at the end of the street so that there was no chance of Mother seeing us.

"Don't forget Sunday," said Father. "I'll be thinking about you all week. Hey! I've just remembered, I've got the house now! Why don't you come there instead? Then I won't need a disguise and we can talk for hours by ourselves."

This seemed a much better plan and he wrote the address down on an old bus ticket which I found in my pocket. (He had a pen but no paper.)

I got out of the car and we looked at each other. I felt myself going red yet again, but he just stared at me with the same astonished look of delight that Mother sometimes gives me. No wonder I went scarlet!

"Can I call you Father?" I asked.

"Of course you can!" he said. "Anything you like, darling. Father, Daddy, Dad, Pops, any of them! They're all music to my ears."

"All right," I said, feeling dreadfully shy all of a sudden. "Good-night then . . . Dad!"

This finished me off completely. Blushing almost purple, I leaned forward and aimed a kiss which caught him on the chin. Then I turned and tore off down the road.

"Good-night, Susie," Father called softly. "Two o'clock Sunday, I'll be sitting by the door. Don't forget!"

"I won't!" I called back, breathless with excitement. "I'll be there."

Father watched through the open window of the car until I had turned in at the gate. I fastened it behind me and leaned out to wave, but the car had vanished silently, like a ghost, or a dream.

CHAPTER FOURTEEN

As I went up the front steps, I thought how strange it must be, to be so rich that you could actually forget that you'd just bought yourself a house. Mother and I still look greedily into the windows of flats with "For Sale" notices and imagine where we would put the furniture and the five-inch thick carpets.

I knew Mother was still up because the lights were on in the front window, which is the sitting-room. I wondered what I would say to her, particularly as I was glowing with excitement, and of course I was dying to tell her! In the end, I decided that it would be best to come clean and just hope that she'd understand.

I let myself in quietly and crept into the hall. I was surprised to hear voices in the sitting-room and very cautiously I pushed open the door.

Zöe's mother was sitting in a chair by the gas fire and Mother was pacing about with tears streaming down her face. I don't know who looked more horrified, Mother, Mrs Rawlings or me. For a second we all froze, then Mother advanced across the room and grabbed me by the arm. Before I had time to think clearly, she began hitting me – all over, but mainly on the shoulders. I was so astonished that I just stood there, and at one point she hit me so hard on the back that I fell on to the floor.

"You *wicked* girl!" she gasped. "You wicked, *wicked* girl! Oh you *naughty* girl. Get *up*!"

She hauled me to my feet and began thumping me again. Of course by this time I was in floods of tears, but she didn't seem able to stop.

"Where *have* you been, Susan?" she demanded, between pushes and thumps. "What on earth have you been *doing* till this time? And why did you lie to me? You know how I feel about lies!"

This thought obviously refuelled her anger for she started shaking me by the shoulders till I felt quite sick. Somewhere in the distance I heard myself sobbing, "Stop it, Mummy! Stop it! Stop it!"

In the end Mrs Rawlings came and gently detached her from me and pushed us firmly into opposite chairs.

"Calm down now, Mrs Hunter," she said to Mother. "At least she's quite safe. I'll go and phone the police and tell them she's back, and make us some tea. I'm sure there's some explanation, isn't there, Susan? Now just you both get your breath back for a few moments."

I curled up on my chair and howled. It was such a horrible end to a wonderful evening. Mother came over and knelt in front of me. She put her arms round me and sobbed as well.

"Susie, Susie. I'm sorry I hit you. I was so relieved, that was all — look, here's a tissue — I've been worried sick. We've had the police out looking for you since nine. I thought you'd . . . I thought you'd been . . ."

Whatever it was that Mother thought I'd been made her burst into tears again.

Mrs Rawlings brought in a tray of tea, and set it down on the table.

"I've rung the police," she informed Mother. "They said they knew she'd turn up and not to worry. Now if you'll excuse me I'd better get back home. Poor Zöe's upset too. She thought you were lost for ever. You are a naughty girl, Susan, worrying us all like this."

Mother took Mrs Rawlings to the front door and I

felt awful when she came back in, with her face all swollen and blotchy from crying.

"Why did you lie to me, Susan?" she asked sternly, sitting down opposite me.

"It wasn't *exactly* a lie," I replied.

"Yes it *was*, Susan," said Mother. "You told me you were staying the night at Zöe's when you had no intention whatsoever of staying there. What I want to know is where were you between 8.15 and now?"

"Just wandering about," I mumbled. I wanted desperately to tell her about Father, but she was so angry I didn't dare in case it made things worse.

"Wandering about *where*?" asked Mother. "For heaven's sake, Susan, don't be stupid. You know that I'd *let* you wander about if you wanted to, but not alone at this time of night. Did you go to Trafalgar Square by any chance?"

"Yes," I answered, wondering how on earth she knew. "I sat up with one of the lions."

"So it *was* you," said Mother. "After I rang the police, they rang back and said that they'd stopped a girl answering your description in Trafalgar Square but she ran off. This gets worse and worse, Susan! Why *did* you run off? Were you waiting to meet someone?"

"No," I replied truthfully. "I was just sitting up there. Please may I go to bed now?"

"No you may *not*," said Mother. "We're getting to the bottom of this, Susan Hunter, if we have to sit here all night."

I started to cry again and thank heaven, the sight of my tears must have moved her to pity.

"Come on then," she said, taking my hands and pulling me to my feet. "Get off to bed. I can't be cross any more, I'm just so relieved that you're all right. But

83

you needn't think you've got away with this, my girl. I shall want a very understandable explanation tomorrow, do you understand?"

"Yes, Mum," I said, diving for the door.

A few moments later, when Mother was saying good night to me, I suddenly thought of something.

"How did you know I wasn't at Zöe's?" I asked.

"Because I went round with your art homework," replied Mother. "You'd forgotten it and I knew you had to get it in on Tuesday so I popped round at nine o'clock. Well of course Mrs Rawlings hadn't the faintest idea what I was going on about, oh I felt such a *fool* when I discovered that you'd lied to me and that you weren't there. Mrs Rawlings woke Zöe and she told us that you'd said something about a quest, but that she'd thought you were coming back here. Oh Susan, I'm so angry with you. We've been running round in circles all night and then in you come without a care in the world at nearly midnight . . . oh, go to sleep before I start again!" She stopped at the door.

"All the angels guard you," she said with a rather frosty smile.

"And you," I answered. "And Mummy, I am sorry. There was a reason."

She turned off the light and I wriggled down under the bedclothes.

The next thing I remember is Mother shaking me awake. For a minute I thought that something else awful had happened, then I saw that it was daylight.

"Wake up," Mother was saying. "It's half past eight! You'll be late for school and I'll be late for work. We've overslept, come on now quickly, out of bed!"

I staggered out of bed and she propelled me towards

84

the bathroom. She was already dressed, and by the time I came out of the bathroom she was putting on her green coat, the one I'd borrowed the night before.

"Oh Susan!" she suddenly exclaimed, holding up the coat. "You could take more care of my things when you borrow them. Look at this. It's got some sort of stain all over the back of it. You know I don't mind you wearing my clothes but the least you could do is look after them."

"Sorry," I muttered.

I pulled on my clothes, bolted a cold cup of tea and a piece of toast, and we fell out of the door together at exactly a quarter to nine. Halfway down the road I remembered the fateful art homework and had to rush back for it. I caught Mother up at the end of the road.

"I'll see you this afternoon," she said. "I want you to come straight to the shop after school and wait for me till we close as I can't trust you to go home on your own."

"Oh *Mother*!" I said crossly.

"Don't 'Oh Mother' *me*!" she snapped. "After last night and with no explanation, I'm surprised you have the nerve to be cheeky to me. I'll see you at the shop after school and that's all there is to be said. Do you understand?"

"Yes, Mother," I replied sulkily.

"Good," said Mother briskly. "Have a good day at school then, darling. I hope Miss Pontin likes your picture. *I* think it's lovely."

Zöe was dying to know where I'd been the night before. We didn't get a chance to talk properly until break, and even then I wasn't sure whether to tell her or not.

"If I tell you, Zöe," I said, "will you promise not to

tell *anyone* at all, not yet anyway."

"I promise," said Zöe solemnly.

"All right then," I said. "You know that programme, the one about the Stranger?"

"Of course I do," said Zöe.

"Well," I continued, "the Stranger, at least the actor who plays him, is my father."

"He *isn't!*" exclaimed Zöe.

"Yes he is!" I went on. "And last night I went to see him."

"You *didn't!*" gasped Zöe, sounding even more astonished.

"I did really," I said. "I went to see him in his dressing-room and then he brought me home in his Rolls Royce."

Zöe looked at me for a moment then she burst out laughing. "Oh Susan!" she giggled. "You are a nitwit sometimes. A Rolls Royce!"

"It *was!*" I insisted, feeling very annoyed. "And I waited in Trafalgar Square and a policeman chased me, and the Rolls Royce had thick, furry carpets. It *did* Zöe, honestly."

"You're just making it up," said Zöe.

"No I'm not!" I retorted.

I won't bore you with the rest of the conversation. We went on like that for ages, and in the end I stormed off in a huff vowing never to speak to her again. As I've already mentioned, I didn't think she'd believe me, but I was still rather hurt that she was quite so disbelieving. I suppose it was my own fault for telling so many tall stories in the past. (What's that story about the boy who cried "Wolf!"?)

When school finished for the day, I made my way to the dress shop feeling awful. I felt even worse when I saw the look on Mother's face as I came in. She looked like an atom bomb about to go off. Even Ruth darted me an odd look from the counter where she was wrapping a pair of trousers for a customer.

Ruth told Mother she could go early, so we left a few seconds after I'd arrived. As we set off, Mother hissed in my ear, "Just *wait* till I get you home!" in the most alarming tone of voice.

"But what — ?" I started.

"Don't talk," said Mother grimly. "Just let's get home."

As soon as we were inside the front door, Mother propelled me into a chair and sat opposite me. We didn't even have time to take our coats off. She rummaged in her bag and pulled out a newspaper which she opened and held up in front of me. My heart sank.

There in the middle of the front page was a huge photo of Father with me in his arms. I could hardly believe my eyes. Then I suddenly remembered all the flashing lights and it dawned on me that they must have been flash-cameras.

The photo showed me with rather a worried look on my face and my arms tightly round Father's neck. Father seemed to have his eyes shut and was smiling. To my surprise, I looked quite nice in the picture with all my hair blowing about, though you couldn't see my freckles or the shape of my nose because the light was so bright. The caption ranted on about Father and the mystery child who came out of the theatre with him. I do wish people would make up their minds whether I look like a kid or an old lady – or better still, stop going on about it altogether!

"Why didn't you tell me about this, Susan?" asked

Mother, a strange hurt look in her eyes.

"I thought you'd be cross," I replied truthfully. "And it was a secret quest of mine. I didn't even tell Zöe. I'm sorry. *Please* don't be angry any more. I didn't mean to upset you, really I didn't. I won't see him again if you don't want me to. I just wanted to see him once and know what he's like, that was all."

Judging from the expression on Mother's face, I thought she was going to start shouting at me again, but instead she began to cry. Her chin went all dimply where she was trying not to, but she couldn't stop the tears and just sat there all huddled up with mascara streaked down her face. I couldn't bear it and rushed to put my arms round her.

"Oh stop it, *please*," I said, in tears myself. "I'll never see him again. Never *ever*. I'm sorry, Mummy, I really am."

"No," said Mother, sniffing hard and rubbing her eyes. "I should be apologizing to you. Of course I'm still angry that you lied to me, but it's quite natural that you should be thrilled to find out that your father is famous. Of *course* you must go and see him if you want to. It's quite wrong of me to have been so secretive, and denied you his company and all the things we could have had if I hadn't been so hard about him. Of *course* you want to see him, he's your own father. Now let's just get two things straight. The first thing is that my main reason for not letting you know about him, was that I didn't want you being ferried back and forth across the Atlantic; you know, six months in America and six months in England and never knowing where you were or which school you'd be at. I wanted you to have as normal a childhood as possible. Can you understand that?" I nodded. "The second thing," she continued, "is no more lies about *anything*. Promise me."

"I promise," I said. "Cross my heart and hope to die."

"That *won't* be necessary," said Mother, attempting a smile. "But just you stick to that promise and there won't be any more trouble between us."

I told her that I was going to meet him on Sunday, and she said that was fine, and now if I didn't mind, she didn't want to talk about it any more.

She really is quite an amazing person. She didn't even ask me what he looked like or what he'd said to me, or anything. You'd think she would at least be curious, wouldn't you?

CHAPTER FIFTEEN

Just after I got to the end of the last chapter, so many things started happening that I didn't write anything down for ages; in fact I would have forgotten all about it if I hadn't been clearing out a chest of drawers and found these five red exercise books. I sat down and began reading, and when I reached the end of the last chapter I felt disappointed that I hadn't carried on till the end of the story (except that I didn't know what the end was going to be then, because it was like a day to day diary).

I must admit that it's difficult getting started again even though there's masses to tell. I suppose the best thing is to start where I left off, with Zöe rushing up to me at school the next day with the newspaper photo.

She was practically hysterical with excitement, and apologies about not believing that my father really was the Stranger. She told everyone else in our class, and I must admit I was quite pleased that they all knew. I would have preferred to have told them myself, but it would have been too boastful, so I was glad Zöe did it for me. Everyone was ever so impressed, and I would have got quite big-headed if I wasn't such a sensible person.

It was a wonderful relief to be able to look forward to Sunday and not have to plot and sneak off. Zöe wanted to come with me but I told her I'd rather go alone the first time. I consoled her by saying that she could come on the next visit if Father didn't mind. Father! After all these years I could talk about my Father. It was heaven.

That evening, which was Wednesday, I began to feel decidedly peculiar — I mean ill, not mad. I'm *never* ill, so I thought I must be just over-excited or perhaps be coming down with a cold, but by the end of the evening there was no doubt about it, there was definitely something wrong with me. My joints all ached and my eyes hurt if I moved them from side to side.

I realized that if I stayed home from school, Mother would say I was too ill to go out at the weekend as well, which would mean missing Father on Sunday. So I staggered in to school on Thursday and Friday, though by Friday afternoon I could hardly stand up.

On Saturday morning, even Mother noticed that I looked a bit strange.

"You're looking very red in the face, Susie," she said, as we had breakfast together before she went off to the shop. "Are you feeling all right?"

"Just a bit tired," I replied.

Well, it wasn't really a lie, was it? I *was* absolutely exhausted. I just didn't mention the fact that I also felt sick, boiling hot and weak at the knees.

"Well," said Mother kindly, "let's miss out on our visit to The Harlequin today. You just have a nice, quiet day at home and don't worry about doing the shopping unless you want to, I can do it this afternoon, all right?"

The minute Mother had gone, I collapsed into bed shivering and shaking with all my clothes on. It wasn't even a cold day, but I was suddenly freezing to death.

Blast! I thought as I curled up in a miserable ball with my teeth chattering. If I can just get through today, I can go and see him tomorrow.

I set the alarm for eleven-thirty to give me plenty of time to get up and do the shopping before Mother

91

arrived home. I usually do the shopping on Saturday, after all it's a bit mean if she's slaving away at work and then has to go and do all our shopping.

It only seemed a few seconds after I'd fallen asleep that the alarm shrilled in my ear. It was already eleven-thirty, I'd been asleep for three hours and now I was so hot that sweat was trickling down my back. Feeling terribly bad-tempered about being ill, I forced myself out of bed. The minute I stood up, I felt as if I was floating off the ground, and prickling waves of cold swept over my shoulders like a shower of stinging rain. It was no good, I could scarcely move, let alone walk to the shops and carry home heavy bags of shopping.

As a last desperate resort I thought a bath might help, so I ran a nice, hot bath with a swirl of pink bath salts. I was taking off my clothes when I noticed with a blast of shock that I was covered in a dense rash of tiny red blotches. Measles! It couldn't be anything else. At this point, I gave up the fight, abandoned the bath and put myself back to bed to await Mother's return.

It *was* measles. The doctor came and confirmed it, though it was only German measles which doesn't take so long to recover from. I didn't know what to do about Father as I only had his address but no phone number.

"What shall I *do*, Mum?" I asked from my sick-bed. "He'll be waiting all *day* for me. He said he'd be sitting by the *door* at two, and I won't turn up. You couldn't just go and put a note through the door, could you?"

Mother frowned. "All right," she said. "I'll go along tomorrow morning. Now stop worrying and try to get some sleep."

Of course I *did* worry. I tossed and turned all night worrying that he might think I'd just gone off the idea of visiting him. The moment it was light, I wrote a letter saying how sorry I was to be ill and that I'd be round to see him the instant I was better.

First thing after breakfast, Mother set off to deliver my note. I noticed that she had put on eye make-up and washed her hair and put on her best clothes, all of which gave me hope that she might actually want to see Father and look nice for him.

"I'll only be half an hour or so," said Mother. "Less if a bus comes."

"Do stay and have a cup of coffee when you get there," I said casually. "Don't worry about me, I'll probably just be asleep."

"Look, Susan," said Mother, "I'm not even going to knock on the door. I'm putting your note through the letter-box and coming straight home, so you can stop scheming, all right?"

"All right," I agreed, smiling.

An hour passed and she didn't come back, and although I was madly imagining them taking one look at each other and falling into each other's arms, I began to feel so tired and aching that I fell asleep.

I had a very odd dream about being invited to a party and Mother making me a dress out of feathers. I waited at a windy bus-stop with the dress all rustling round me, but when the bus arrived and I got on board, the conductress said that she wouldn't give me a ticket unless I had my hair cut! Having announced this, she produced a huge pair of gardening shears and sliced it all off with one snip. I was so appalled, that I squeezed out of the window and flew away. It was a lovely sensation and I remember thinking that I must be able to fly because the dress was made of feathers!

I woke up with a jolt and saw Mother creeping out of the door.

I glanced sneakily at my watch and saw that she'd been away for three hours!

"Hello," I said.

"Oh, hello," said Mother. "I thought you were asleep."

"I was," I replied. "Did you see him? Was he there?"

To my relief, she smiled at me. "Yes, he was there," she said.

"And have you been there all this time?" I asked eagerly.

Mother burst out laughing. "Honestly, Susie," she giggled, "it sounds as if *you're* the mother and *I'm* the daughter! Yes I was there for at *least* two and a half hours, *and* I was brought home in the Rolls Royce."

"Oh, Mother," I said, "he *is* nice, isn't he, don't you think? He's such good fun, and I heard the girls at the theatre saying that he never drinks at *all* any more, and that was the only thing wrong with him, wasn't it? Well if he doesn't drink now, then there's nothing to worry about, is there?"

Mother laughed and shook her head at me in mock despair. "I gave him your note," she said, "and he was very sorry and said he'd come and see you this evening. He's already had German measles so he won't catch any of your germs."

"Why don't you ask him to stay to dinner, Mummy?" I asked. "*I* won't be much company this evening, stuck in bed, and you can't really invite him round without giving him anything to eat, can you? Or you could go *out* to eat, or to the pictures, or . . . just stay in," I ended up lamely.

Mother snorted with laughter, and doubled up in a

fit of helpless giggling such as I hadn't seen her have for ages.

"I expect we'll find something to do," she said. "Now you really must try and rest for a while. You *are* supposed to be ill, you know."

Of course I didn't go back to sleep. How could I, when my mind was whirling like a merry-go-round.

CHAPTER SIXTEEN

It was just getting dark when I heard the doorbell ring
and then they both came into my room. Father looked
even bigger than I remembered with the collar of his
sheepskin coat turned up and a long, ancient-looking
red scarf with a rather clumsy orange darn in it. He
was carrying a huge parcel wrapped in gold paper
which he shoved into my arms.

"I'm sorry you're not well," he said, unwinding the
scarf and throwing it on the bed. "I hoped this might
cheer you up — open it!"

Opening presents in front of people always makes
me feel a bit shy, you know the way everyone just
stands there and watches you to see if you'll be pleased
with whatever it is. I took off the paper very carefully
(I save wrapping-paper to use later for Christmas and
birthdays because it's so expensive) and there inside
was an amazing nightdress case.

It was a pierrot doll all dressed in white satin with
black bobbles down the front and a beautiful, sad face
crowned with a tight black hat.

"Oh he's lovely!" I gasped with delight.

"Look inside," said Father.

I unzipped the back of his costume and took out an
even more amazing nightdress. It was made of electric-
blue material with tiny yellow moons, silver stars and
white clouds embroidered all over it like a magician's
robe.

"Oh it's *wonderful*! They're both wonderful. It's the
best nightie I've ever —"

I stopped myself in horror as I realized that I was

wearing my new nightdress that Mother had made for me. The material was the old bathroom curtains which were thin blue towelling (frayed at the edges but all right in the middle) and Mother thought they would make a nice, warm nightie for the winter. She's not very good at making things, and it had taken her weeks of stitching, unpicking and cursing before she'd finished it, and even then one of the sleeves was so tight at the armhole that it practically cut off my circulation. I felt awful.

"It's *very* nice," I said again. "I'm lucky to have *two* special nighties, aren't I?"

Mother laughed. "Oh, Susie," she said. "It *is* absolutely beautiful. You don't have to be so worried about my feelings all the time. Why, if I had a choice between the botched bathroom curtains and that . . . creation, I know what I'd choose. You've got the most tactful daughter in the world, Lloyd, did you know that?"

Suddenly she leaned over and picked up the scarf from my bed. "Hey," she said "This isn't – ?"

"It *is*," nodded Father. "How could I throw it away when you made it for me? Look, I even darned it myself when it got a hole."

"Oh, Lloyd," said Mother. "You are a sentimental old idiot. Anyway, I'll bet you hired some minion to darn it."

"No I did not!" said Father indignantly. "I'll have you know that I do all my own mending – of personal treasures anyway, *and* I can still cook a splendid meal when I want to. Tell you what! Why don't I cook you my special bacon-and-bits risotto? I haven't done that for years."

"There isn't any bacon," said Mother.

"Who cares?" said Father. "We'll have a bits risotto

97

then. Come on, you must have *something* in the kitchen."

So they settled me with my lovely presents, and a carrier-bag full of comics and books that Father had brought as well, and off they went to the kitchen chatting happily.

I hope you don't think I'm awful, but I couldn't resist creeping out of bed to have a little listen and make sure they were getting on all right.

"Don't bring her presents *every* time, will you, Lloyd?" Mother was saying as I pressed my ear against the kitchen door. "It's very nice when she's ill, but we really have been very poor – yes I know we needn't have been – but we *have* been, and she's such a nice kid, I'd hate her to get spoilt and grabbing, after all this time."

"Of course I won't," replied Father. "The last thing I'd want to do would be to change her for the worse. I've brought a little something for you too as a matter of fact, that's if you're sure it wouldn't make *you* too spoilt and grabbing."

"Oh, Lloyd," murmured Mother, sounding embarrassed. Then I heard a package being ripped open. I winced as I heard the paper tearing; it really *kills* me the way people just rip up perfectly good wrapping-paper.

"Oh it's beautiful!" she exclaimed. "Oh it's *really* beautiful, Lloyd. Shall I put it on now?"

I was nearly going insane with curiosity. What was it?

"Yes, go and try it on," said Father. "I bought it to fit the you I knew ten years ago. Maybe you've got bigger."

"I certainly have *not*!" said Mother indignantly and I

heard her advancing towards the door. Quickly, I staggered back to bed. It would have been awful if Mother and opened the kitchen door and I'd fallen into the room.

Later on, they brought me some of the bits risotto, and Mother was wearing "it". It was a blue dress which looked as if it must have been made especially for her. The material actually floated as she moved, and there was a sort of cardigan, only very romantically styled to go with it. She looked like a princess.

What an evening! Although I was ill, it was so full of presents and promise, and I fell asleep feeling thoroughly happy, which in my experience is a very rare way to feel.

CHAPTER SEVENTEEN

I couldn't wait to get back to school and tell Zöe all about Father visiting and the presents, but the day I went back she wasn't there. Guess what? She was at home in bed with German measles, caught no doubt from breathing in all my germs. Still, at least I could go and see her with all my news and the books and magazines that Father had brought when *I* was ill.

Come to think of it, it's just as well I *did* get ill because Mother would never have gone to see Father if I hadn't been bed-ridden, and to my great surprise, after that first evening they just teamed up. Father rang each night from the theatre and arrived each Sunday, and sometimes he came late at night in his flashy car after the show.

My heart zoomed to the ceiling one day when I asked Mother why Dave didn't come round any more and she replied, "I think your father would be hurt if I was seeing someone else."

She cared! She cared that Father would be hurt. Maybe, *maybe*, oh I didn't dare imagine too much!

It was difficult going out with Father on Sundays because he really was pursued by *Worlds Apart* fans wherever he went. At first I was rather thrilled to be with him when everyone started nudging each other and then rushing up for autographs, but very soon it just got annoying when we wanted to have a quiet cup of tea in a sandwich bar, and they wouldn't leave him alone.

Still, we managed to go out on the Heath a lot – we found a very real false beard and wig which made us shriek with laughter when he first wore it, but it *did* mean that we could wander about as we pleased.

Zöe came with us sometimes, I didn't want her to feel left out, and I even took Father to our secret den and showed him the matchbox with the Quest inside. (I burned it later as I had vowed at the start.) He was fascinated, so I told him all about the den, and about my beloved Loki. He didn't think we were silly and seemed to understand perfectly all our nutty goings-on.

As the weeks passed by, Zöe and I began to change. I don't know why – well I do really; it was the other girls at school. They all seemed so much older than us and they often sneered at us and called us babyish. We had a lot of fun poked at us, and it was worse for me now that everyone knew about my dad.

Honestly, people can be so horrible sometimes. I mean, *we* weren't nasty to them, in fact we tried quite hard to be nice all the time. Anyway, in the end it began to change the way Zöe and I felt about everything.

When we went out on the Heath together, neither of us had the heart to whistle the dogs, and if one of us did (usually me) the other would accuse them of being childish, so gradually we just stopped having them at all and we didn't visit the den any more; *I* did, by myself, and sometimes I even had a good cry while I was there. I cry an awful lot these days, even when I'm quite happy. It's funny, isn't it?

One day Zöe came in to school with her hair cut off. I nearly had a heart attack, but do you know, she looks a lot prettier with it short.

I'm not cutting mine though. Father asked me not to, he said it looks just right. Actually, I have found a really nice way of wearing it. If I plait it in about fifteen plaits overnight, it all stands out in ripply waves the next morning and looks very dramatic. It takes hours to do all the plaiting and just as long to take them out again, but it's worth it.

Christmas hoved into sight so I began madly making everyone's presents. For Mother, I made a mobile out of blown eggs. It nearly drove me out of my mind trying to attach cotton to the eggs as they break very easily. I painted a different bird on each egg. There were ten altogether and I won't list them all, you'll be relieved to hear! Anyway, I was very pleased with it and packed it very carefully in a shoebox, wrapped with one of my saved bits of wrapping-paper.

For Zöe, I made a family of hedgehogs to fit inside a matchbox. I made them out of a special clay that doesn't need firing and they took hours of fiddling about, but somehow they didn't look very much for a best friend, so I included a blue and white striped T-shirt that she's always borrowing. It suits her better than me anyway.

Father was a problem. He's so rich that it was difficult to know what to make him – he's got everything. In the end I made him a pair of slippers out of the remains of the bathroom curtains. I embroidered his initials on the front part, but they looked a bit odd because the initials on the left foot got a bit out of hand and trailed over the side. Also, I had to use about four thicknesses of towelling and they looked more like oven gloves than slippers by the time I'd finished; so I included a little note explaining what they were. I was careful not to wrap them up in the gold paper. That's the only trouble with using old wrapping-paper, you have to remember who gave it you. People would be offended if you gave them back their own wrapping-paper!

There were only two weeks left till Christmas. Mother and I hung up decorations all over the flat. They were the same ones we'd used for years. Long paper chains, twirly streamers and crinoline ladies whose skirts opened out. The Christmas tree, which was an old green artificial one, had fallen to pieces in its box, so we bought a lovely new silver one on a red stand and I made new decorations for it.

The flat looked beautiful, like a fairy cave. In fact, the only trouble with Christmas is that you have to take all the decorations down on January the sixth and everything looks drab and boring again. Why can't flats and shops look bright and glittering all year round?

One day, just before Christmas when Mother was at work and I was on my own at home drawing (my hand from all different angles, I'm hopeless at hands), Father rang up and asked to meet me on the Heath. I was surprised as it was a freezing cold day, and lately he hadn't been seeing me much during the week because he'd been busy.

"Where shall I meet you?" I asked.

"At your den," said Father. "Three o'clock on the dot, OK?"

"OK," I agreed, pleased but puzzled.

I pulled on my new coat, — I haven't told you about my new coat, have I? Well, you just won't *believe* this. It's like a sheepskin duffel coat. Brand-new, beige sheepskin with a hood and toggles and such a thick furry lining that you could go out in your underclothes in a snowstorm if you were wearing it! I felt a bit rotten showing it to Zöe because her family couldn't

103

possibly afford one like it and we've always worn the same sort of clothes before. Still, she doesn't seem to mind. That's because she's a true friend and she's pleased when nice things happen for me, as I would be for her.

As I tramped over the Heath towards the den, I suddenly felt really sad that I couldn't conjure up Loki any more. I *tried* to, but he just wasn't there. To think I actually used to hear the bushes rustling and see him bounding towards me. It made me feel old and grown-up, the way Zöe and I always vowed we would never be.

I rounded the corner and saw the familiar clump of bushes ahead, and I realized how I didn't even creep stealthily up to the entrance in case anyone saw, the way I used to. All the magic had gone and Father hadn't arrived yet and I felt really sad.

"Loki," I called softly, just for old times' sake, and then (and I've been dying to tell you this bit) something quite astonishing happened.

I heard a rustling coming from the den, a *real* rustling, and something came bounding out of the entrance and nearly knocked me over with big puppy paws. It was a gigantic puppy, a wolfhound, with a sweet bright face and amber-coloured eyes.

I really did think I must be dreaming it seemed so unbelievable, but then again, the frantic furriness of the creature and my face all wet from being licked felt unmistakably real. I decided that it must be just an extraordinary coincidence.

"Come here, boy," I said. "Let me see your collar. Who do you belong to then, eh? A big chap like you out on your own?"

I turned his collar round and looked at the engraved disc.

LOKI, it read clear as day.

I turned it over, and there on the other side was my name and Father's address. The penny began to drop and I looked around to see Father crawling out of the den.

"I'm glad you were on time," he said, jumping to his feet and brushing sticks and leaves from his jacket. "We were beginning to freeze to death in there. Do you like him then?"

"He's wonderful!" I said. "Thank you so much, and look, he likes me! But I won't be able to keep him at the flat. They won't allow pets at all, not even cats and I couldn't smuggle him in because he's so big. Are you going to keep him at your house? Is that why you put your address on his name tag?"

"Nope!" said Father, smiling secretly. "*You're* going to keep him at my house."

For a horrible moment I thought that he must be trying to get me away from Mother to go and live with him.

"Oh I couldn't possibly leave Mother," I said. "Not even for you and Loki. She'd be so dreadfully hurt. It's not that I don't love you too, but —"

"You won't have to leave her you lunatic!" laughed Father. "You don't seriously think I'd try to lure you away from Pet, now, do you? Your Mother's coming too. You're *both* coming to live with me – at my house – all together."

This was almost too much to take in.

"Really?" was all I could squeak.

"Really," agreed Father. "Pleased?"

"Of *course* I'm pleased." I said. "Will you get

105

married again?"

Father laughed. "Well, *actually*," he said, "we won't have to get married again. We still are. We never got divorced, odd though it must seem — I suppose you could call it the longest trial separation in history. We'll have a party though, to announce that we're back together, and I'll have to tell the press or you and Pet will be hounded all over the place."

"Will we all go and live in America when the show finishes?" I asked.

"No," said Father. "We're going to stay right here, at least till you've finished your schooling. Your Mother tells me that you've settled down well there, and you'll still have Zöe, so it won't be too different for you. I've had enough of *Worlds Apart* anyway. It's good money, but there are so many other things I'd like to do.

"I've had such a time with that puppy. I got him weeks ago, but I had to wait till ten days after his second distemper injection before he could set his delicate paws on the Heath. Today's the first day he's been allowed out. I had to hide him away in the furthest room every time you came to visit me. You've got to train him now, so he's as good as the other Loki or you won't enjoy him."

"Oh I will!" I said.

"Come on then," said Father. "Let's go home for some tea before we get frostbite. Your Mother's waiting at my house — I mean *our* house — and she's dying to know how you felt when you saw your dog. She wanted to come too, only we wouldn't both fit in the den."

So off we went, and the wintry sun disappeared into a bank of yellow-grey cloud, and Father pulled up the

106

hood of my coat and put his arm round me, and Loki bounced along beside us on springs; and that seems the best place of all to end this story, with a real, proper HAPPY ENDING before we get round the next corner and something dreadful happens!

THE END

APPENDIX

P.S.

CHAPTER EIGHTEEN

(I couldn't decide which sounded best!)

Actually there are a few more things that happened after the day I got the real Loki.

First of all Mother gave up the job at the shop and has gone back to being an actress. She's a bit worried because she knows she'll be given work because she's Lloyd Hunter's wife. On the other hand, as she pointed out, she'll have to be extra good or the critics will pull her to pieces.

Then there's my room. It's totally perfect, it really is. It overlooks the Heath and there's all trees outside the window and I was allowed to choose everything for it myself. I've got this apple-green carpet that's about five feet thick (well, two inches) and a bed on a platform with a curtain round it, and a box for Loki underneath, and a desk sticking out at the end. The curtains are bright yellow, so it always looks sunny in the mornings even when it's raining. Oh yes, and there's an armchair that turns into a bed, so Zöe can stay the night.

Father is just as nice as I thought he would be and we all get on very well, but the funny thing is, and you're going to think I'm absolutely bonkers when you hear this, sometimes I miss the way it used to be, you know, just Mother and me on our own. I even miss our dingy little flat, and The Harlequin on Saturdays, and the old lady who lived upstairs who used to bash on our ceiling if we played music too loud. It's silly, isn't it? I mean, most of the things I miss weren't even particularly nice, but I still miss them.

Then at other times, when I'm feeling all pleased and at home in the big, new house, I suddenly get worried that it's all been too quick! Perhaps Mother will go off him and she'll come and tell me to pack because we're leaving and she doesn't want to hear any more about it.

Not that there are any signs of that, far from it. They haven't even had a row yet.

Right, that's enough! I've done it again haven't I? There was that nice neat HAPPY ENDING and I've waffled off into another chapter. The thing is, if I'd told you about my room and Mother giving up her job *before* the part where I got Loki, you would have known what was going to happen, and it wouldn't have been a surprise.

So perhaps now, you could go back and read the last chapter again and finish at the proper ending.

I don't know! I'll never get the hang of writing books. I mean, how do you *end* the thing when there's always so much more to add? I'll just have to be firm and say goodbye.

"Goodbye!"

IN AT THE SHALLOW END

Hannah Cole

For Dawn, it's nerve-racking enough to be visiting a dad she hasn't seen for years – but when he arranges swimming lessons, the holiday looks like turning into a nightmare. For though her sister Lisa takes to swimming like a duck to water, Dawn hates it and stays rooted in the shallow end. But, as she eventually discovers, even in the shallow end there can be challenges...

"Wise, humorous and entirely delightful... Beautifully written." *The Junior Bookshelf*

THE TIME TREE

Enid Richemont

Rachel and Joanna are best friends and the tall tree in the park is their special place. It's Anne's too. So it hardly seems surprising that the three girls meet up there – except for the fact that four centuries divide their lives.

"Ms Richemont develops her story beautifully, with finely controlled writing and clear delineation of her three main characters." *The Junior Bookshelf*

MORE WALKER PAPERBACKS
For You to Enjoy